"You really are the dumbest smart man alive, aren't you?"

Morgan glowered as the full meaning of what she'd said settled in.

"When I'm shamelessly throwing myself at you, the least you can do is make a halfhearted attempt to catch me."

Stunned, he asked, *"What?"*

"You heard me," she retorted petulantly.

He wondered how long it had been since he'd really wanted anything, anyone, and he wasn't sure now that he ever really had before this, and that was a startling discovery at his age.

"I can't keep doing this!" he told himself as much as her.

She huffed out a sigh of pure disgust. "I would like to know why not."

"Simone, I am not the man for you," he stated flatly.

"I think you are."

"I'm too old."

"Ha! I think not."

Shooting up to his feet, he began to pace. "Then put it another way. You're too young."

She tucked her chin and rolled those big, beautiful eyes up at him. "Surely you can do better than that."

ARLENE JAMES

says, "Camp meetings, mission work and church attendance permeate my Oklahoma childhood memories. It was a golden time, which sustains me yet. However, only as a young widowed mother did I truly begin growing in my personal relationship with the Lord. Through adversity He has blessed me in countless ways, one of which is a second marriage so loving and romantic it still feels like courtship!"

After thirty-three years in Texas, Arlene James now resides in Bella Vista, Arkansas, with her beloved husband. Even after seventy-five novels, her need to write is greater than ever, a fact that frankly amazes her, as she's been at it since the eighth grade. She loves to hear from readers, and can be reached via her website, www.arlenejames.com.

The Bachelor
Meets His Match

Arlene James

HARLEQUIN® LOVE INSPIRED®

Recycling programs
for this product may
not exist in your area.

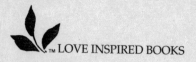 ™ LOVE INSPIRED BOOKS

ISBN-13: 978-0-373-81771-9

THE BACHELOR MEETS HIS MATCH

Copyright © 2014 by Deborah Rather

www.Harlequin.com

Printed in U.S.A.

But we have this treasure in jars of clay to show that this all-surpassing power is from God and not from us. We are hard pressed on every side, but not crushed; perplexed, but not in despair; persecuted, but not abandoned; struck down, but not destroyed.

—*2 Corinthians* 4:7–9

For Marge Tracy

You prayed this one through, my dear.
I thank you for that support.

Invaluable.

Chapter One

"Oh, Professor Chatam, I was *sooo* hoping to get an appointment as your teaching aide."

Morgan smiled warily at the young woman batting her eyelashes at him and gave his pat answer. "I only hire male teaching aides. It's school policy. Male professors hire male aides. Female professors hire female aides. It's entirely fair because we maintain gender parity among our professors."

The pretty, if somewhat showy, brunette folded her arms and stuck out her bottom lip. "Awww. Isn't there something I can do for you? You wouldn't have to pay me."

Morgan stiffened his smile. "I can't think of a thing. But thanks for asking."

Gideon Modesta, the chair of the School of Theology at Buffalo Creek Bible College, came to the rescue, clapping a hand on Morgan's shoulder. "Great party, Morgan. As usual."

Nodding to the young lady, Morgan closed the lid on the grill that he tended on the patio of Chatam House, the antebellum mansion owned by his aunties, triplets in their seventies, and turned to face his good friend.

"Thanks, Gideon. I'm glad you're enjoying yourself."

"But of course. Your graduate student mixers always start off the new semester happily."

The disappointed female student finally turned and melted into the throng of young people and faculty chatting beside the pool. Gideon chuckled.

"Poor child has no idea that rule about teaching aides was instituted for your benefit. Must be tiresome being the campus heartthrob year after year."

"Oh, stop," Morgan chided as Gideon mopped his beaded brow with the towel draped about his neck. It might be the second day of September, but the daytime temperature, true to central Texas, hovered at ninety-four degrees. "I'm forty-five years old. For most of our students, that makes me positively ancient."

"In other words, only half of the female population at BCBC is now in love with you at any given time," Gideon said drily. "What a terrible comedown for you. How do you bear up?"

Morgan replied in kind. "I indulge my worst habits, of course. I climb on the fastest motor with two wheels I can find and hit an oval track. You'd be amazed how speed can blow the cobwebs out of your mind and narrow your priorities."

Gideon grimaced. "What you need is a wife. Not only would she put a stop to that reckless streak of yours, she'd lay out your priorities for you. Mercedes says it's time to serve those burgers, by the way."

Morgan laughed. Everyone knew that Gideon's wife, Mercedes, gave her husband little rest and also that they adored each other. He looked to his fellow cook, Chester Worth, the majordomo at Chatam House. Chester checked his watch, nodded.

"As usual," Morgan said, lifting the lid on his grill to poke at the beef patties with a spatula, "Mercedes is right." Waving the spatula over his head, Morgan shouted, "Chow's on!"

As students, department heads and spouses began lining up, he slid a thick, char-grilled patty of juicy beef onto the bun and plate that appeared in Gideon's hands, then handed a spatula to one of his department professors so the serving could go twice as quickly. Hilda, the cook and housekeeper at Chatam House and Chester's wife, joined her husband in dispensing burgers from his grill. When all of those in line had been served, Morgan transferred the remaining hamburger patties to a warming shelf before calling for quiet.

"Let's give thanks."

In moments, all had grown still and bowed their heads. Morgan spoke a short prayer, thanking God for those present, the fellowship and the food. He asked God for a special blessing for his generous aunts, then requested that God guide students and educators alike, performing His will in each of their lives, to His glory and honor, before closing in the name of Christ Jesus. After a chorus of amens, he checked the buffet table and saw that the iced tea jug was running low. Good. It would give him a moment of peace and quiet away from the bustle of the party.

Cordés Haward, the diminutive provost of BCBC, stopped him at the door, laden plate in one hand and glass of lemonade in the other. "It's good of your aunts to open their house to us for this fete," the small middle-aged man said, the black eyes bequeathed him by his Puerto Rican mother sparkling. He saluted the distant figure of Morgan's aunt Hypatia, as spry as ever in her mid-seventies, with his lemonade.

Morgan chuckled. "You know how they feel about the college."

"Indeed, I do. What blessings they have been to us."

"I'll be sure to tell them you said so." With that, Morgan pushed open the multipaned glass door and passed into the cheery sunroom. A long, narrow space filled with greenery and colorful tropical-print cushions that softened the sturdy bamboo furniture, the bright area could be warmed by a large rock fireplace at one end, so it was used year-round as a breakfast room.

As Morgan moved toward the butler's pantry that separated the sunroom from the kitchen, he saw a young woman sitting quietly at a glass-topped table, nursing a disposable cup of lemonade. Slight and pale, with short, spiky reddish-brown hair, she had the biggest, most soulful gray eyes that Morgan had ever seen. Set beneath horizontal brows in an oval face with a delicate, pointed chin, a small, plump mouth and a short, straight nose, they were the color of an overcast sky. Something more than her obvious beauty made Morgan look twice—an aloneness, a solitude set her apart from the others in a way that the walls of the sunroom could not. Arrested by the sight, he found himself at a standstill. He could not, in fact, seem to go forward again without engaging her somehow.

"Heat too much for you?" he asked conversationally.

She tilted her head in noncommittal reply, the slender column of her neck seeming too delicate to support the weight of her pretty head, and ran a fingertip around the rim of her drink. She was young, obviously a student, but she didn't dress like the other girls in grungy, low-slung jeans and layered tanks or bathing suits and sarongs. He took in the neat white capris and simple shapeless pale green collared blouse that she wore buttoned to the throat, the long sleeves rolled to her elbows, tail untucked. Though of good quality, her clothing seemed too large for her.

Even her white leather sandals swallowed her dainty feet. Mystery wrapped around her like a shroud, but it was her cool self-possession in the face of his obvious perusal that truly intrigued him. He tried another conversational gambit.

"Not swimming?"

She shook her head, keeping her glance on the table in front of her.

"If you need a suit, I'm sure we have extras. I could ask."

Meeting his gaze calmly, she said, "No, thank you. I'm fine." Her voice had a husky quality to it, almost a rusty sound, as if she didn't use it very often.

He tried to place her among the underclassmen who had passed through his lecture hall and couldn't. Stepping forward, he put out his hand, aware suddenly of its size. At an even six feet in height and a firm if lanky one hundred and eighty pounds, he wasn't exactly a giant, but next to her he felt like one.

"I'm Professor Morgan Chatam."

She smiled wryly, as if secretly amused. "Yes, I know."

He dropped his hand. "How is it that I don't know you, then?"

"I recognize you from your online lectures."

"I see. So, you're a remote student."

"I was."

He backed up to lean against the tall table behind him. "Well, are you going to tell me your name?"

That luminous gray gaze met his. "Simone Guilland."

Simone Guilland. She gave the name a French pronunciation, *Gi-yan*. Of course, Simone Guilland of Baton Rouge. The name brought two facts to mind. One, she was a member of his advisory group. The second troubled him: her entrée into the graduate program was conditional upon her completion of his History of the Bible undergraduate course, a course in which Simone Guilland had enrolled remotely and then dropped *after* the deadline. Normally, as department head, Morgan had to approve for reenrollment any student who had dropped a class under such circumstances, but in this case, he hadn't even been given the option.

"I have you now," he told her lightly. "You dropped the course in the middle of a project, as I recall."

"Yes. I was sorry about that."

"You left your teammates in a bad spot," he pointed out.

"It couldn't be helped," she told him, her flat inflection implying that he shouldn't expect any explanation, but then he hadn't gotten an explanation from the provost, just the last-minute instruction that she had been provisionally admitted to the graduate program and enrolled in his History of the Bible section for this fall semester. Whatever had happened, her admission had been approved by the highest echelon at the university. He couldn't help being curious, however, and as her adviser, he was entitled to some answers.

"I believe you're from Baton Rouge, Louisiana. Is that correct?"

"I moved here from Baton Rouge."

"Funny, you don't sound much like Baton Rouge."

"And have you spent a lot of time in Baton Rouge, Professor Chatam?" she challenged.

She had him there. "One visit only."

Her small smile of victory proclaimed that Simone Guilland was not as fragile as she appeared.

"You must go again sometime. The Guilland family is old and storied in the area. I'm sure you would find your visit interesting."

"Perhaps I will." Why the next words fell out of his mouth, he would never know, but he heard himself say, quite suggestively, "Perhaps you would induce your family to give me a personal tour?"

She froze, simply stopped, as if everything about her—her heart, her pulse, her breath, her thoughts—simply switched off. Then, abruptly, she switched on again. She turned her head and stared through the glass wall at the busy patio and pool beyond, saying calmly, "I haven't spoken to any member of my family in years. We...fell apart. Our connections just disappeared."

"I am sorry," Morgan murmured, assuming that

she was one of the foster children he'd seen come through BCBC over his lengthy tenure there. Removed from their families for any number of reasons, they were often among the hardest working and the most motivated and successful students. They frequently required counseling and extra help, however.

"Tell me, Ms. Guilland, what are your goals, your plans?"

She lifted her chin. "I'm not entirely sure. I'd like to work with the homeless in some capacity, so I'm taking an advanced degree in social services."

She slid from her chair and went to lean against the cold rock fireplace. He was surprised to find her taller than he'd expected, maybe five and a half feet. She made a pretty picture standing there against the rustic backdrop of pale, rough stone.

"You have a lovely home," she said, smiling slightly as if to disguise the fact that she'd changed the subject.

Morgan chuckled, letting her get away with it. "I don't live here. My aunts own the house, which was built in 1860. They're triplets, by the way. My aunts, that is."

"Triplets." She shook her head. "I don't think I knew that."

She wouldn't, of course, not being a local. Nodding, he smiled. "Hypatia, Magnolia and Odelia. They've lived here their whole lives and are universally adored, especially by the family."

For the first time, Simone Guilland truly smiled, showing him a set of white, even teeth and pert apple cheeks. For just an instant, those cheeks struck a chord in him, a memory of a memory, something he couldn't place. Then she whispered, "That's lovely," and he felt a flush of...something.

"They're lovely," he told her, feeling as thrilled as he did at the end of a race. "Kind, dear Christian ladies. They've made Chatam House a haven. I can't tell you how many they've taken in." He cleared his throat and rushed on. "Just recently they gave a home to the family of some longtime friends and household staff."

"Oh?"

Naturally that would interest her, given her concern for the homeless. He mentally congratulated himself. He pointed through the glass to Hilda and Chester.

"The Worths have been with my aunts for, oh, twenty years or more. Hilda is the most amazing cook. Anyway, when Chester's brother died recently, my aunts moved his widowed daughter and her children into the house. She married my cousin Phillip." He chuckled again, thinking how often that sort of thing seemed to happen at Chatam House. "They started a business together, and—" He broke off, realizing that Simone had straightened away from the fireplace, a pained look on her face. "Is something wrong?"

"Died?" She put a hand to her temple. "Y-you're saying that, um…Chester's brother…"

"Are you all right?" Morgan asked, edging forward.

She shook her head as if to clear it. "Sorry. I—I seem to have bees in my head. Guess I should've eaten. Um, did…did I hear that correctly? He *died?*"

"Yes. Chester's brother, Marshall, died," Morgan muttered, moving closer.

She swallowed audibly. "And, ah, you said something about his daughter being a widow?"

"With three kids," Morgan confirmed offhandedly, watching Simone as she swayed. "But not anymore. She married my cousin Phillip last month."

Simone smiled slightly and nodded. "I see. Sorry. It's…confusing." Then her eyes simply rolled back in her head, and she melted like hot wax left too near a flame.

Morgan leaped forward, catching her in his arms before the back of her head could connect with the edge of the stone hearth. It was like catching smoke. She felt weightless, boneless.

Scooping her up, he rushed outside with her, shouting, "Need help here!"

People swarmed them. Going down on one knee, he dropped her on a quickly vacated chaise lounge. His aunts appeared at his elbows, and Chester handed him a towel that had been dipped in the pool.

"What happened?" Uncle Kent, his aunt Odelia's

rotund husband, asked as Morgan wiped Simone's face with the wet towel.

"We were just talking and she fainted."

A retired pharmacist, Kent knew a bit about medical matters, so when he told someone to get her a soft drink, something with sugar in it, Morgan simply added, "And put some food on a plate. She said she hadn't eaten."

Already rousing, she moaned. Morgan wiped the wet towel over her face again, taking away the makeup that had concealed the freckles across the bridge of her nose and the dark circles beneath those gorgeous eyes. Suddenly, Morgan wanted to shove away everyone else and hold her close. He told himself that she was just a kid, no more than twenty-one, probably, and a student, strictly off-limits for a professor. That was a line he had never crossed, one he had never even been tempted to cross, despite ample opportunity over the years. Until now. But why?

She had already proved herself untrustworthy, having dropped a class after the deadline and leaving her project teammates in the lurch. She had likely been a foster child and could well be anorexic, given her frailty and lack of eating. Moreover, she seemed to be a loner and something of a mystery, probably one of those kids with a tough past that she hadn't quite left behind. He should have wanted to wash his hands of her, right then and there, but as her adviser and host he was responsible for her to a point, and until he was satisfied that she was well, he couldn't relinquish supervision of her. More to the point, he didn't want to.

It was that simple and, alas, that complicated.

Died. The word seemed to reverberate inside Simone's skull, echoing so loudly that her eyeballs bounced. She blinked, realized immediately what had happened and opened her eyes to find herself face-to-face with the much too handsome Professor Chatam. He ran a hand through his damp, nut-brown hair, his cinnamon eyes crinkling as he smiled.

"Welcome back," he said, sounding relieved. The smile cut grooves in his lean cheeks and flattened the fascinating cleft in his chin. Add a high, smooth forehead, the long, straight blade of his nose and a square jawline, and she could simply find nothing to dislike in that face.

Gulping, Simone sat up a little straighter and glanced around.

The kindly faces of three older women smiled down at her. All three had gently cleft chins. The one they called Hypatia wore a silk pantsuit, a string of pearls and pumps. To a pool party. Her silver hair had been swept into a sleek, sophisticated roll on the back of her head. Her sister Magnolia, on the other hand, wore trousers and rubber boots with a gardening smock, her steel-gray hair twisted into a grizzled braid. The third one—Odelia, Simone thought her name was—could have worked as a sideshow in a circus. The plumpest of the sisters, she wore her short, white hair in a froth of curls tied with a multicolored scarf that matched the rainbow print of the ruffled caftan. She accented this with stacks of bangles at her wrists and beads at her throat, as well as clusters of tiny rainbows that dangled from her earlobes.

"How are you?" asked the rainbow-festooned Odelia.

Simone managed to croak, "Fine."

"Look at me," Morgan Chatam commanded. Simone automatically bristled, but she fought back the impulse to snap and complied. "Have you fainted like this before?"

She considered lying but decided against it. She'd put such things behind her, so instead she nodded and cleared her throat. "I'm all right now."

When she started to swing her legs to the side, however, he placed his hands on her shoulders and pinned her back against the chaise.

"Not until you answer a couple of questions."

Her heart thunked with uncertainty. She hadn't had a moment to think since she'd learned that her father had died, and this handsome man was making it difficult to order her thoughts. A plate of food hovered beside his head, and she glanced up at the familiar woman who held it. Had she been recognized, then? Now that it was too late? Simone had expected it upon her arrival, but when it hadn't happened, she'd started to plan how to make herself known, then to realize that her father was dead…dead. She shivered uncontrollably.

"Is this the result of an eating disorder?" Morgan demanded. "Anorexia? Bulimia?"

Her brows jumped up, a short, almost silent laugh escaping her. "No."

He considered, relaxed, dropped his hands and finally reached up for the plate of food. "You won't mind eating this, then."

She was hungry, so she didn't argue. Taking the plate warily, she relaxed somewhat when Hilda, who happened to be her aunt by marriage, turned away without so much as a second glance. Not recognized, then. She supposed she had changed a good deal in the past nine, almost ten, years, and given the ravages of cancer… Simone sometimes wondered which was worse, the disease or the cure. She turned off the thought and smiled her thanks at those around her.

"This is exactly what I need." She picked up the burger and bit into it. "Mmm." After chewing and swallowing, she touched her fingertips to the corners of her mouth and said, "I prefer my cheeseburgers with mayonnaise."

Chuckling, Morgan Chatam pushed up to his full height. "Mayo coming up."

"And a napkin, please."

"And a napkin."

While he went off to fetch those things for her,

she turned to sit sideways on the chaise. Her uncle Chester handed her a soft drink, nodding and moving off without so much as a glimmer of identification. Simone felt a pang of disappointment, but perhaps it was for the best. She couldn't think of that now. The Chatam ladies stayed with her until Morgan returned with his own meal in hand. As they moved off, he sat down beside her, placed his drink on the ground and handed her a plastic knife, indicating the glob of white on his plate.

"Mayonnaise." While she slathered the condiment onto her hamburger bun, he plucked paper napkins from a pocket and dropped several into her lap. "And napkins."

"I thank you." She bowed her head at him, adding, "And I apologize. I forget to eat, and I don't always get as much sleep as I should."

"And that's all it is?"

"It's certainly not an eating disorder," she said with a wry chuckle, adding, "It probably didn't help that I walked over here in the heat."

"In that case," he said, "I'll be driving you home."

"Oh, that's not nece—"

"I'll be driving you home," he repeated, making it clear that the matter was not open for discussion.

She subsided at once, but it rankled. At twenty-six, Simone had been on her own for almost a decade. If anyone could claim the title of "adult," then she could. She certainly wasn't proud of being the black sheep of the family. She had run away from home at the tender—and stupid—age of sixteen, but she had survived. It had been a near thing at times, and she wasn't always proud of how she had managed, but no one at the college needed to know that. Her family was another matter.

She'd intended to confess all to her dad and hope, trust, that he could forgive her. He'd been good like that, always willing to extend another chance. Her mother had seen that as weakness, and to her shame, Simone had, too, but she'd learned otherwise over the years. Now that it didn't matter.

Grief loomed. She shoved it away. She had no right to it. Later, she would decide what to do.

After eating most of the food she'd been given, she shook her head and handed over the plate. "That's all I can manage."

Morgan Chatam stacked the plate atop his empty one and set both on the end of the chaise. "Good enough. Perhaps you'd like to go inside where it's cool now and rest for a bit."

"That sounds great."

She got to her feet, as steady as could be. He lifted a hand and she preceded him back to the house, saying, "About that cousin of yours, the one who married the widow…"

"Phillip? What about him?"

"You said something about a business."

"That's right. Smartphone apps."

Simone couldn't help smiling. Yes, that sounded like her sister, Carissa. Tom, Carissa's husband—*first* husband—had studied computer science, and Carissa had always been fascinated by the subject. Poor Tom. It was hard to believe that he, too, had died.

"And do they live around here? Phillip and...his wife?"

"They do. They bought a house and set up an office less than a mile away."

"That's nice."

She and Carissa had never been the closest of sisters, but Simone was glad to know that Carissa was doing well. Now that their dad was gone and Carissa had married into the Chatam family, however, she wasn't likely to want her black sheep little sister around, especially if her full history should be uncovered. And it surely would be. The Guillands, her in-laws, had uncovered it quite easily.

After that, nothing could convince them that she was good enough for their precious son. "A diseased street kid" who could not even give them the grandchild they so desperately wanted was not a fit wife for the Guilland family heir. Simone didn't really blame them for having her marriage to their son annulled, any more than she would blame her sister for turning away from her in shame. So why even give Carissa the chance? Why put Carissa through that?

It seemed to Simone that even her dreams of home and reconciliation had died.

Chapter Two

Morgan reached around Simone to open the sunroom door. "Let me show you someplace comfortable to wait out of the heat."

"All right."

He led her through the sunroom and down a darkened back hallway to a large room filled with comfy overstuffed furniture and a large flat-screen TV.

"The family parlor," he said. "There are video games, if you're interested."

She cut a glance at him, quipping, "That's not what I expected to hear. Then again, you're not exactly the typical college professor."

He laughed. "You just haven't seen me in my tweed jacket with the suede patches on the elbows."

She smiled at that. "Sounds rather old school. Seems to me that college professors these days are either eccentric or ultraprofessional types."

"Well, history professors are a different breed."

"Yes, but you don't fit that mold, either."

He grinned and for some reason that he couldn't explain even to himself, he prodded her for a personal opinion. "No?" He spread his arms then folded them. "How would you label me, then? Be kind, now."

She narrowed her eyes at him, obviously trying to size him up, and he was aware of his heartbeat beginning to accelerate. "If I didn't know and had to guess, I'd say…race car driver."

His jaw dropped, but he quickly snapped it shut again. She had to be putting him on, of course. His predilections were well-known around campus.

"That's funny." He laughed, but it sounded forced even to his own ears. "But it's motorcycles. Not race cars."

"You're kidding."

He didn't appreciate her attempt to play stupid. Oddly disappointed, he turned and walked out. Everyone knew that speed was his greatest weakness, his great indulgence. Sports cars, motorcycles, fast boats, even roller coasters were his idea of FUN, writ large and in capital letters. Some of his family gave him a hard time about it, but he was skillful, careful and respectful of the laws, saving his true exploits for the racetrack. Next to moving fast, he liked tinkering and kept a fleet of vehicles, one for every purpose. More than one young miss had tried to use his fascination with horsepower to spark a more personal fascination. That this one appeared to take the opposite approach somehow unnerved him.

Then again, everything about her unnerved him, and he couldn't quite figure out why. He'd been struck by the sight of her sitting alone at that table in the sunroom. Then, when she'd passed out, dropping right into his arms…he'd never quite experienced anything like that. It hadn't been panic, really, or even shock; it was more…a heightened awareness, a deep physical connection overlaid by concern for her well-being and something else he could only describe as *possessiveness*. He didn't like it. He didn't like it at all, but something about Simone Guilland drew him. Hopefully, she hadn't noticed.

He kept an eye on her, wandering in and out of the house regularly. She didn't move from the couch. A few others went inside and joined her, making use of the video games he'd spoken of earlier. She chatted with them and cheered them on as they played, her husky voice seeming to deepen with use until the sound of it flayed his skin like velvet lashings and set his nerves on edge.

The party began to break up about dusk, as it was meant to. As usual, many hands made short work of the cleanup. Morgan could always count on his faculty in the History Department to pitch in and help. With Hilda and Chester overseeing everything, they were finished in no time at all. Still, dark had descended by the time he escorted Simone out to the two-seater parked beneath the porte cochere on the west end of the house. He'd treated himself to the Valencia-orange convertible when he'd made department chair last year. The BMW Z4 was a sharp, fast, classy bit of self-indulgence for which he refused to feel guilty. He worked hard, after all, tithed religiously, gave generously and spent what was left as he pleased. Simone dropped down into the passenger seat, her eyebrows rising, and fastened her safety belt as he strode around the front end to take his place behind the steering wheel.

"Am I going to regret this?" she asked cheekily.

He couldn't help grinning as he put the transmission in gear. "Nope. I am, if I do say so myself, an excellent driver."

"Modest, too," she quipped, then she laughed outright at his look of dismay. He found himself laughing with her. He *was* rather proud of his driving skills.

After backing out, he drove the sports car sedately down the looping drive and south through town the dozen or so blocks to the university district. She directed him to a three-story boardinghouse on the north edge of the university campus. It was a ramshackle place, some forty or fifty years old. Once a dignified family home, it had long ago devolved to seedy, its large, airy rooms broken into small cells with common bathrooms on each story and a central living space and utilitarian kitchen on the ground floor. The yard had been paved over to provide parking, and bicycles and skateboards crowded the warped porch.

Morgan had been inside many times. While single men and women were never allowed to share living space in buildings on campus, the school had no control over off-campus housing. Typically, these three-story boardinghouses hosted men on the top story and women on the middle one, with the bottom floor reserved for common rooms. These places tended to be loud and run-down and catered to the poorest students living on the smallest of stipends. Just now, loud music poured from the building.

"We have a resident praise band," she said wryly, explaining the music.

"No wonder you haven't been getting much sleep."

She shrugged. "They're good people, and this is all I can afford on my wages."

Morgan hated to think of quiet, physically fragile Simone here. However spunky she might be, he sensed shadows and sadness in her, trouble and need. It was his job to help her, if he could. That's what faculty advisers at Buffalo Creek Bible College did. He'd had his share of troubled students. Christian colleges were not immune from the ills of society; perhaps the effects were mitigated somewhat, but the world was still the world, and Christians still had to cope with it. If she had been raised through the foster care system, as he suspected, he might be able to find resources for her of which she was unaware.

"Where do you work?"

"At the Campus Gate Coffee House."

He knew it well. The proprietors were friends, and he ate breakfast there at least once a week. Located just across the street from the west gate to the campus, it was a very popular place.

She reached for the door handle, saying, "It doesn't pay much, but when I've finished school, I won't owe a dime to anyone."

"Well, that's a definite plus," he told her, "but perhaps you should think about applying for a grant or a small loan."

She shook her head. "That's not for me." With that she let herself out of the car, saying, "Thank you for the ride, Professor Chatam."

Morgan frowned at the way she dismissed his suggestion so casually, but she was already moving away from the car. "Take care of yourself," he called. "See you in class on Wednesday."

"I'll be there," she promised, waving as she hurried up the walk to the house.

As he drove away, Morgan made a mental vow to keep track of her. He wasn't yet convinced that she didn't have an eating disorder. He'd seen bulimia more than once, not usually in young women from foster homes, though. He'd hate to see something like that derail Simone's education—and it wouldn't do to let an inappropriate attraction distract him from his duty. That wouldn't do at all.

Simone closed the flimsy door of her shabby room and sagged against it. The beat of the bass guitar echoed up the stairwell from the floor below and throbbed inside her aching skull. The narrow bed against the far wall called to her, but she went to the laptop computer atop the rickety desk in the corner and turned it on. That, a pair of low, sparsely filled bookcases, a small lamp, a trash can, an oval rug, a pair of curtains and a desk chair comprised the furnishings of the room. It was little to show for nearly a decade, but such things had ceased to matter to her in a hospital bed in a cancer ward in Baton Rouge.

Without Morgan Chatam to distract her, she could no longer contain her need to know what had happened to her family. A simple internet search brought up her father's obituary on the computer screen.

Marshall Doyal Worth, fifty-seven, had died on June 20 after a long illness. An old photo of him as a young man, one of her favorites, accompanied the text. Survivors included his mother, listed as Eileen L. Davenport Worth; his older brother, Chester; sister-in-law, Hilda; two daughters, Carissa, of the home, and Lyla—no residence mentioned—grandsons Nathan and Tucker; granddaughter Grace; a niece and a nephew; and several great-nieces and nephews. Marshall had died, it would seem, from cancer, as it was requested that memorials be made in the form of donations to fund research.

Obviously, cancer ran in the family.

At least Carissa and her children had been living with Marshall at the end, so he hadn't been alone. Tears flowed from her eyes as Simone folded her arms across the edge of the desk and lowered her aching head to pray.

"Oh, Lord, I'm sorry. Please tell my daddy that I'm sorry. It's too late. I left it too late. I thought I was doing the right thing by coming here now, but maybe I shouldn't have done it. Show me what to do now, and forgive me. Please forgive me."

She had more than nine years of "forgive me" stacked up, nearly a decade of penance to pay and mistakes to undo. And now it was too late. With her father gone, what was the point in coming here? Carissa wasn't likely to want anything to do with her now.

Poor Carissa, to have lost Tom and then to have nursed their dad through cancer all on her own.... No, Carissa wasn't likely to want anything to do with her wayward little sister now. And who could blame her? Tom had been Carissa's high school sweetheart. She'd never showed any interest in any other guy. How tough it must have been for her to lose him!

Simone lifted her head and looked up Tom's obituary. Four years. He had died in an accident of some sort more than four years ago.

Her tears became sobs of grief and shame and regret. Once started, she couldn't seem to stop them, not even when she impulsively looked up the wedding announcements in the local newspaper and saw a photo of Carissa and her beautiful children posed with a tall, ruggedly handsome, dark-haired man with the Chatam cleft chin. Carissa looked a little older, more capable, healthy and quite stunning.

"Mr. and Mrs. Phillip Chatam," the caption read, "and family."

The article beneath detailed that the couple had been "united in holy wedlock" on Friday, August 8, at Chatam House, the home of the groom's aunts, by the groom's uncle, Hubner Chatam Jr. Maid of honor was Dallas Chatam, sister of the groom.

Simone felt a pang at that. She had been the maid of honor at Carissa's marriage to Tom, but she hadn't been here when Carissa had buried Tom or their father or when she'd married Phillip Chatam. Simone hadn't even known that she had a niece and nephews. Carissa had been pregnant when Simone had left, but she hadn't given that much thought at the time. All things considered, that was probably best. Simone tore her gaze away from the photo of the children and continued reading.

Asher Chatam, brother of the groom, had served as best man. The bride was given in marriage by her uncle, Chester Worth. The happy couple's parents were listed as the late Marshall Worth and Alexandra Hedgespeth and the doctors Murdock Chatam and Maryanne Burdett Chatam.

"Hedgespeth," Simone murmured, swiping ineffectually at her tears. That was a new one. She couldn't help wondering how many other last names and husbands her mother had claimed in the past nine years.

Simone hadn't expected life to stand still in Buffalo Creek while she was gone. It certainly hadn't stood still for her. But she hadn't expected *this*.

Her dad had been only fifty-seven, and Tom had been in his thirties. So young.

Fresh tears gushed from her eyes. She cried for her father, for her late brother-in-law, for Carissa and her children, but she refused to cry for herself. She knew only too well what her dad must have suffered and could only hope that Tom had not suffered anything similar. What Carissa had endured Simone could only imagine. At the same time, Simone prayed, hoped, that Alexandra had not spent the intervening years flitting from man to man, demanding that everyone stop and think of her, put her needs and desires first. Yet that new last name, Hedgespeth, suggested that her mother had not mended her self-indulgent ways. That meant that Carissa had, indeed, dealt with it all alone.

Could Carissa ever forgive her only sister for abandoning her to deal with such tragedies and their demanding mother alone? The very question so smacked of their self-absorbed mother that Simone vowed never to ask it. She had no right to ask it, no right to dump her problems and failures on the sister who had stayed to do what a good daughter should.

Carissa had happily remarried. She didn't need a prodigal sister turning up to complicate her life just when things were going well for a change. No, it was too late for that.

It would have been better if she hadn't come to BCBC and Buffalo Creek, but what was done was done. Aaron, her former husband—if he could be called that—had paid her tuition in full, just as she'd requested. It was all Simone had asked for in the settlement, a college education, and his cagey parents had seen to it that the funds they'd dispensed to be rid of her could not be used for any other reason. She had specified Buffalo Creek Bible College, and that's where they had sent the money, so this was where she would have to attend school. That meant she would just have to keep to herself.

If her own aunt and uncle hadn't recognized her, then it wasn't likely that anyone except those closest to her would, at least not in her present condition. She saw no reason, then, for anyone to equate Simone Guilland with Lyla Worth—no one, that was, except her sister and mother. Those two alone might recognize her, so she would just have to keep her distance from everyone connected to either of them. That included the kind, charming and debonair Professor

Morgan Chatam, even if he was her faculty adviser and she had to take his class.

It was a pity that she couldn't take Professor Chatam's course online again, but school policy made that difficult because she'd dropped it before without explanation. That hadn't seemed important at the time, given the severity of the circumstances. Once she'd understood that she was moving to Buffalo Creek and would have access to the BCBC campus, she'd simply accepted that she would take the course in person. She hadn't known then, of course, what she knew now. Still, all she could do was keep her distance and let Carissa live her life without worrying about her foolish baby sister.

Her decision to remain incognito made, Simone sat in the back of the class on Wednesday and tried to blend in with the eager young students around her.

She needn't have bothered. Professor Chatam's warm, cinnamon-brown gaze nailed her the moment he strode into the room. He wore that tweed jacket with the suede elbow patches about which he'd teased her, but he immediately shrugged out of it and slung it over the back of his desk chair, rolling up the sleeves of the tan pinpoint shirt that he wore with a brown tie and brown slacks. His hair seemed lighter than she'd remembered, a medium golden-brown with glints of silver, brushed straight back from the slight widow's peak in the center of his high forehead. He took a pair of gold, half-frame reading glasses from a pocket and slid them onto his nose. Suddenly, the cleft in his chin seemed more pronounced, more compelling.

Before, at the party, he'd appeared engaging, urbane, a tad dangerous and undeniably attractive. Now he had a commanding air about him. At once authoritative and yet affable, he looked devastatingly handsome. Every girl on campus probably had a crush on him. Simone ducked her head.

Thankfully, he wasted no time in getting down to business. She'd admired his easy, informative style on his recorded lectures, but that paled in comparison to his classroom persona. Morgan Chatam, professor, held a class of seventy students rapt, imparting knowledge with such facility and precision that it became obvious he had been born for this. He didn't just lecture, he engaged, using banter as well as media to get his points, facts and ideas across. At times, everyone seemed to be talking at once, yet he never lost control of the lecture hall, not for an instant, and he seemed aware of what everyone was doing all the time.

His memory proved phenomenal—that or he'd done some research on her since he'd seen her last. It would be flattering to think that it was the latter, so she didn't dare, not that he gave her time.

"Ms. Guilland had an interesting observation on that point," he said when the subject turned to a particular discussion item. Then he accurately quoted what she had written in an online chat. At the same time, he invited her to elucidate with a gesture of his hand. She cleared her throat and voiced her thoughts. Nodding, he moved on. She tried not to feel pleased when the students around her glanced her way with something akin to admiration, scribbling furiously as if her thoughts were important.

He hailed her as she followed the throng to the door at the end of class. Unlike other professors, he'd arranged his lecture hall so that the students filed past his lectern. "Simone, how are you feeling?"

"Great. Just great."

"No more fainting?"

"No. I'm fine."

"Stay that way."

"I plan to."

Parked on the corner of his desk, he flashed that suave smile at her and nodded. She turned away, wishing that her heart wasn't beating just a little faster than it ought to and that so many others weren't following the brief conversation with such avid curiosity. The last thing she needed was speculation about her and a man, any man, but especially a Chatam. She'd had enough trouble with men in her lifetime. What she needed now was to forget that the male of the species existed. Moreover, she had to keep her distance from the Chatams and anyone else with a connection to her sister and family. All she wanted, all that was left to her, was to finish her education and make a difference in this world.

The chaplain at the hospital in Baton Rouge had told her that she had a destiny to fulfill in Christ, and she believed it with all her heart. Why else would He spare her life when all hope had seemed lost? Perhaps when He was done punishing her for past mistakes, He would make His purpose known to her. Until then, she would just have to bear up under the pain of her father's death and the losses she had dealt herself with her own foolish, selfish behavior.

Anyone who knew Morgan Chatam well would list observation and a keen intelligence among his key virtues, so when Friday showed the opposite of marked improvement in Simone Guilland's condition, he noticed. Her carefully applied cosmetics no longer fooled him in the least, and the neat tailoring of her cotton slacks and matching print blouse failed to disguise the fragility of the slight form that he had so effortlessly carried in his arms only days earlier. As before, she chose a seat in the rear of the room, and as before, he let her know that she was on his radar. This obviously irritated her, and that wore his much-vaunted patience surprisingly thin, so he decided to take a direct approach, asking her to stay after class.

She didn't like it one bit. Those gray eyes stormed as she stood quietly before his desk. He let her stew a moment before dropping his glasses onto the desk blotter and leaning back in his chair to peg her with a level gaze.

"What's wrong?"

"Don't ask me. You're the one who seems to have a problem."

She was a cheeky miss, not at all impressed by his consequence. He heaved a silent sigh, toying idly with the glasses.

"Are we going to play games, or are we going to be adults about this?"

That pointed little chin ratcheted up a notch. He might have smiled if the impulse to do so hadn't alarmed him so. As it was, the beauty of those plump lips and that stubby little nose and those enormous gray eyes troubled him at the strangest times. He couldn't afford to be enamored of her chin as well, not to mention her streak of stubborn independence.

"Adults mind their own business, Professor Chatam."

"Which, as your adviser, is exactly what I'm doing, Ms. Guilland. There is something wrong with you, and I mean to find out what it is."

He wanted Simone Guilland's problems, whatever they were, solved; otherwise, he feared she would give him no peace.

She stared him straight in the eye, as immutable as the Sphinx, neither confirming nor denying, simply giving away nothing. He tried a different tack.

"Simone, I'm not your enemy. You have no reason to fear me."

Yes, I do.

Though unspoken, he saw it clearly in her eyes and on her face just before she turned and headed swiftly to the door.

There she paused and glanced back, softly saying, "Thank you, but I'm as fine as I can be."

As fine as I can be.

Morgan gnashed his teeth. Well, that was just not good enough.

Chapter Three

Rising, Morgan gathered his things and walked through the building to his department suite. His administrative assistant, Vicki Marble, sat at her desk downloading online syllabi to see who had completed the week's reading and first assignment, due by midnight. They did everything electronically these days, which cut paperwork in half and quadrupled computer time.

"Hey, Morg."

"Vic. What are the girls doing this weekend?"

"Shopping for prom dresses."

"All three of them?"

"All three of them."

"Give my condolences to Dwight. He's a better man than me. Three teenaged daughters." He gave a shudder just to see Vicki laugh. Redheaded, freckle-faced and as plain as a mud fence, she seemed to have been born good-natured and laughing, as well as efficient and organized. Her husband and astonishingly beautiful daughters adored her. "Speaking of Dwight," he said, "I need a favor."

"Name it."

Dwight Marble worked in the provost's office, handling admissions. Morgan explained what he needed then went into his office, closed the door and sat down at his desktop computer. Quickly, he brought up Simone's complete file.

She was older than he'd assumed—twenty-six as of the twentieth of this past August. She had completed her undergraduate work—all but his class—in Colorado and via remote study in Baton Rouge. Her next of kin was listed as Laverne Davenport Worth, whose address was in Fort Worth. The name Worth struck a chord with him, given that Hilda and Chester Worth comprised two-thirds of the staff at Chatam House. The name was fairly common in the area, however, and he'd never heard any mention of a Laverne, so he discounted any connection, especially when he read that the Guilland family, of Baton Rouge, had paid Simone's tuition in full, for the entire course of her graduate degree, via an unusual trust account.

Morgan sat back in his chair with a thump. He had seen scholarships and endowments of every variety, but he'd never seen anything like this. What on earth was going on here? He decided that he'd be eating breakfast at the Campus Gate Coffee House, where

Simone worked, bright and early the next morning, and at some point he was going to have a frank discussion with Simone Guilland.

How much he looked forward to that breakfast at the Campus Gate Coffee House troubled Morgan all that evening. He told himself that he was just doing his duty by pigeonholing Simone Guilland, but he couldn't quite convince himself. He'd gone to greater lengths for other students. Why, he'd driven one young man all the way to California and enjoyed a delightful summer respite with his aunt Dorinda Latimer and her family while he was at it. Still, he'd never lain awake in the night picturing another student's face or remembering how his heart had quivered with the flutter of her eyelashes as she'd regained consciousness after he'd carried her limp body in his arms.

He was quite put out with himself by the time he tucked his newspaper under his arm and slid into the Beemer around nine the next morning. He'd meant to be up and about earlier, but his restlessness had made for a late night. Besides, by his estimation, the coffee shop shouldn't be too busy on a Saturday morning.

Wrong. The place was popping when he arrived, so much so that he had to park around the corner and walk nearly a block. All of the al fresco tables were taken, he noted as he pushed his way inside and caught the eye of the owner and manager, Frank Upton. He'd hoped to have a quiet word with the fellow. Instead, he got a nod and a point in the direction of a tiny table at the end of the bakery counter where Frank usually did his paperwork.

"Be glad to visit if you have a minute."

"Sure. If I have a minute."

Shaking his head, Morgan walked over to the table. A cup of steaming-hot black coffee and a small cruet of cold cream laced with cinnamon appeared almost as soon as he sat down. He smiled at the waitress, Frank's wife, Loretta.

"Simone will be over to take your order in a moment."

"She's here, then?"

"Simone? Yes. You know her?"

"She's one of my students. Tell me, is she all right?"

Loretta shrugged her ample shoulders. "I assume so. She's a quiet one, never complains. Gets right to work. Stays busy. She's awfully tired at the end of her shift, but that's not surprising, a little thing like her."

"I hope that's all it is," Morgan muttered, opening his newspaper.

Loretta went off to manage the coffee counter, and presently Simone showed up, clad in blue jeans, a bright orange T-shirt and a yellow apron.

"Professor Chatam." She produced an order pad from an apron pocket. "What can I get you?"

"I'll have one of those crusty cinnamon muffins and a couple hard-boiled eggs."

"Coming right up."

She swept off, returning moments later with a gargantuan muffin and two peeled eggs in a bowl.

"Loretta says the coffee is on the house," she said, slapping down the ticket.

"It always is," he told her with a smile, hoping to engage her in a moment's conversation, but she was off again before he could explain that he and Frank had been friends since high school.

He drank his cup down and signaled for a refill, which she promptly delivered, then she was off again, her slender arms laden with trays bearing plates filled with food. Morgan tried to read his newspaper, but he couldn't help being aware of her as she zipped around the room, which became even more crowded as the hour wore on. Morgan ate his eggs and his muffin and read his newspaper, but Frank didn't find a moment to leave the till or Simone a minute to chat.

Just at the point of giving up, Morgan folded his paper and drained his cup for the final time when he heard a crash and an exclamation. His heart leaping, he somehow knew what had happened. He didn't remember getting to his feet or crossing the room; he would never understand how he knew where to look for her among all the tables and people, but suddenly he knelt beside Simone's crumpled form. Like a puppet whose strings had been cut, she lay sprawled and bent, her joints at odd angles. Her dark, chestnut-brown eyelashes curled thick and long against the pale orbs of her cheeks. She had a delicate, wounded look, her short hair wisping about her face.

"Simone," Morgan whispered, his heart in his throat, but she didn't so much as flutter an eyelid. "Call an ambulance," he instructed in a loud voice. Then he pulled out his own phone and dialed Brooks Leland, his best friend and the finest physician he knew.

As the phone rang, he prayed. *Let her be okay. Please, Lord, let her be okay.*

After insisting that the good doctor leave a patient to speak to him, Morgan filled Brooks in on what he knew of Simone's physical situation, which wasn't much. Then he badgered Brooks into meeting him at the emergency room. By the time he'd convinced the doctor to abandon the patients waiting to keep their appointments and walk across the street to the hospital, the ambulance had arrived and Simone was rousing. Morgan forbade her from so much as sitting up then waved over the emergency medical personnel.

It seemed to him that they took their precious time getting the story, checking her vitals and loading her into the ambulance, but eventually Morgan found himself following the ambulance to the hospital in his car. No sooner did they arrive, however, than Brooks Leland threw Morgan out of the examining room. Not only that, he refused to discuss the first thing about the case with Morgan, citing HIPAA laws. Morgan couldn't believe it.

"I called the ambulance! Well, I had it called. I've been with her twice when this happened."

"Doesn't matter. You're not family. You're out."

Horrified and angry, Morgan called Simone's next of kin after getting the number from the college. The number turned out to be a place called Pleasant Acres, a retirement home or perhaps even a nursing home, from the sound of it. But they weren't giving out any information, either. All they would tell him was that Laverne Worth couldn't come to the telephone. Morgan decided against leaving a message at that time, hung up and paced the waiting area until Brooks deigned to summon him.

A few years younger and a couple inches taller than Morgan, Brooks wore lab coat and stethoscope, white tie and tails or blue jeans and boots with the same easy aplomb. Shocking silver temples and eyes the color of Spanish gold set off his dark, wavy hair. Fit, unfailingly pleasant and hardworking, Brooks was a hard man to hate, as Morgan well knew.

"What is going on?" Morgan demanded, relieved to see Simone sitting up on the gurney, color once more returned to her cheeks.

She looked away, leaving explanations to Brooks. Morgan parked his hands at his waist, waiting. The doctor leaned against the tiny counter behind him, crossed his legs at the ankle and folded his arms.

"We've reached an agreement, Ms. Guilland and I. She needs rest, good nutrition and time."

"She'll get it," Morgan promised, just as if he had a right to do so.

Brooks smiled and looked down at his toes. "She needs to take a *minimum* of two weeks off work."

"I did not agree to that," Simone stated calmly, shaking her head. "I have rent to pay."

Morgan ignored her, saying, "She'll move in with my aunties."

"No!" Simone erupted. Both men ignored her, for she couldn't possibly understand how often the Chatam sisters took in needy guests.

Brooks nodded, saying, "That did occur to me. And when I say a minimum of two weeks, I do mean that as a bare minimum. Four or six weeks would be better."

Simone shifted on the gurney. "I cannot possibly—"

"She's been working at the Campus Gate," Morgan told Brooks. "I'll speak to Frank and Loretta as soon as I get her settled at Chatam House."

"You'll do no such thing," Simone insisted. "I can't possibly quit my job and move in with your aunts."

"You can," Morgan told her firmly, "and you will if you want to stay in school."

Those storm-gray eyes blazed fire at him, but Morgan just turned his attention back to Brooks.

"Her condition won't prevent her from attending classes and mastering her studies, will it?"

Brooks shook his head. "No. She can manage school, if she takes care of herself."

Morgan felt a rush of relief, but it was short-lived as he realized that something was, indeed, wrong with her. He moved to the side of her bed and took her hand in his. "Can't you trust me now with whatever is ailing you?"

She tilted her lovely head, but then her gaze fell away and she reclaimed her hand. "I keep telling you, I'm fine. I just need time."

Morgan folded his arms. "All right, have it your way, but you're coming with me to Chatam House, and that's final."

"It really is the best solution," Brooks put in.

"Not for me," she argued hotly.

"Yes, for you," Morgan assured her. "My aunties have taken in many strangers in far more troubling circumstances, believe me."

"You don't understand," Simone told them. "I cannot go to Chatam House."

"It's Chatam House or the hospital," Brooks said bluntly. "Look, you'll have plenty of privacy, excellent food and all the time you need to regain your strength. What more could you ask for?" He pulled a prescription pad from the pocket of his lab coat and went on briskly. "Now then, I'm going to write you a couple scrips. One, the blue pills, I've already given you, and you'll start to feel the effects soon. You'll only need those for a few days. They'll help you rest. The other we've already discussed." He began scribbling away on the pad.

Simone groaned as if she bore the weight of the world on her slender shoulders. It was all Morgan could do not to gather her into his arms and croon words of reassurance, but BCBC had strict policies about the conduct of professors and students, particularly when it came to professors *with* their students. If she moved into Chatam House, though, the aunties could take care of her, and he could relax.

Maybe then he could get her off his mind once and for all.

The waiflike creature her nephew Morgan ushered into the front parlor had intrigued Hypatia Chatam from the first moment she'd seen him cradling the young woman in his arms nearly a week earlier. She appeared exhausted if not actually ill and quite achingly beautiful.

"Take this chair," Morgan said to her, all but bullying the child onto the gold-on-gold-striped seat of the occasional chair before the fireplace. Except, of course, she was no child, this Simone Guilland, but a woman, however slight and fragile, and Morgan, unless Hypatia missed her guess, was quite struck by her. Interesting. And worrisome.

Morgan was a confirmed bachelor and had been

since his former fiancée had broken their engagement and married his best friend. Hypatia mentally cataloged all the ways that Simone Guilland differed from Brigitte Squires Leland. Brigitte had appeared fit and wholesome, a tall, lithe, shapely woman with long blond hair and cornflower-blue eyes. A nurse, Brigitte had laughed readily, bantering with Morgan and Brooks like one of the boys but remaining very much a lady. She'd been a woman who seemed to know her own mind and heart. What a pity she'd broken off her engagement to Morgan and married Brooks.

Hypatia had thought for sure that would be the end of a lifelong friendship, but Brigitte's death just over two years later had brought Morgan and Brooks together again. To Hypatia's knowledge, neither of them had been seriously involved with another woman since. Now here stood Morgan, hovering over delicate, dainty, big-eyed Simone as if he'd protect her from the whole wide world.

"Magnolia, dear, would you ask for the tea tray?" Hypatia said, deciding that a bit of sustenance would do them all good with lunch still some time away. Despite giving her a sour look, Magnolia went off as asked. Their sister Odelia had accompanied her husband, Kent, on a visit to his great-grandbaby and their great-niece, Marie Ella, the daughter of Kent's granddaughter Ellie and her husband, Asher Chatam, their nephew. They weren't expected until after the normal luncheon hour, so the sisters had agreed to hold back the midday meal. Hypatia made small talk with Morgan until Magnolia returned to take a seat on the settee across the piecrust table from her.

"Now, then, Morgan, Miss Guilland, to what do we owe the pleasure of your visit?"

"We've just come from the hospital, Aunt Hypatia," Morgan informed her, "and Brooks says that Simone must have rest, good nutrition and peace and quiet for at least two weeks, and preferably six."

"Oh, dear!" Magnolia exclaimed.

"It's a great deal of bother about nothing, I assure you," Simone said quickly, sitting forward on her chair.

Morgan sent the girl a quelling glance. "She fainted again."

"It was a busy morning. I've had a stressful week. Things will settle down."

"Her rooming house is one of those noisy, crowded conversions just off campus. One of those praise bands that plays at the campus chapel lives there. You know the sort."

Hypatia couldn't help smiling, as God must smile whenever those young people lifted their raucous music in praise of Him. "I do indeed." She looked to her sister then, understanding what was needed now. "I imagine they practice all hours of the day and night." She looked to Simone, smiling. "It must be great fun, but you can't be getting much sleep."

Simone opened her mouth as if to protest, but she obviously couldn't deny the truth of the matter. Finally, she said, "I don't want to impose on anyone."

Magnolia snorted. "Don't be silly. We have ten bedrooms here, and that doesn't include the carriage house, where the staff live. A quiet little thing like you will hardly be noticed. Our last guests were a lovely lady and her three children. Now, *they* made themselves known."

"And we grew so fond of them that we decided to keep them," Hypatia added. "Our nephew Phillip married the lady, you see."

Simone ducked her head. "I heard that, yes."

Hypatia sent a twinkling glance at Magnolia. "I think the east suite is the most private, don't you?"

"A suite?" Simone yelped.

Magnolia pursed her lips, obviously onto Hypatia's little ploy. "I don't suppose she has any use for two bedrooms, though," Magnolia mused. "The bed-sit combo beneath the attic stairs ought to work just fine."

"Oh, yes," Simone chimed in eagerly. "That sounds fine."

Hilda came in with the tea tray just then, allowing Hypatia to hide her smile of satisfaction. Simone seemed to shrink in on herself, but she perked up again after the tea was poured and Magnolia passed her a plate filled with finger sandwiches, cookies and Hilda's famous ginger muffins. Simone nibbled at first, but once Morgan sat down next to Magnolia, filled a plate for himself and got to talking, Simone quickly ate everything on her plate and drained her cup without even realizing what she was doing. It was obvious to Hypatia that Simone hung on Morgan's every word, as so many of his students did. Was a crush developing? When she sat back and swiped a hand across her brow, however, Hypatia felt a curl of a different kind of concern.

"I think it's time our new houseguest took a nice, long nap."

Morgan set aside his plate and rose at once. "Let us take you upstairs."

Simone nodded, a sign, to Hypatia's mind, of just how weary and weak she was. The girl rose and walked toward the door, thanking Hypatia and Magnolia.

"You're very kind."

"It's our pleasure to be kind," Hypatia told her. Both she and Magnolia rose to follow along. "It's just across the foyer and up the stairs."

"I—I don't have anything with me," Simone said as she crossed the parlor and then the foyer.

"That's quite all right," Hypatia said. "I'll be glad to loan you some things until you can pack your bags."

"I'm really not planning to stay for long," she murmured at the foot of the stairs, looking up at the ceiling.

"We'll leave that to God, shall we?" Hypatia suggested gently, smiling at the blue sky, wafting clouds, fluttering white feathers and the suggestion of sunshine that the unknown artist had created on the vestibule ceiling overhead. She looked down in time to see Morgan nudge the girl, a hand under her elbow.

Simone sucked in a deep breath and started to climb. After only four or five steps, she faltered, bowing and gulping for breath.

"I'm sorry. I seem to be light-headed all the time lately."

She took another step and another, sinking lower with each one. Magnolia placed a hand on Hypatia's arm, and the sisters traded glances.

With the next step, Morgan swept Simone up into his arms.

"I can walk," she protested feebly. "Just give me a few minutes."

"Hush," he told her, climbing the stairs steadily.

Again, the sisters traded looks. Morgan was a scholar, a mature, disciplined, moral man with a strong calling, but a man, nonetheless, and very much a man, obviously.

Simone looped an arm loosely about his neck as they made the turn in the staircase, but she didn't seem to have the strength even to hold on. Her head lolled against his shoulder.

"I'm so sorry," she said in a husky voice. "I thought I could manage. I really did."

"Hush," Morgan told her again. "Just relax."

"Pills," she mumbled. "Must be the pills."

"Take her to her room," Hypatia instructed as soon as they reached the landing. "I'll meet you there in a moment."

Rushing to her own room in the suite that she shared with Magnolia at the front of the house, Hypatia grabbed a pair of her own pajamas and hurried across the upstairs to the combination sitting room and bedroom tucked beneath the attic stairs, overlooking the patio and pool. Morgan had set down Simone on the royal-blue velveteen sofa, his back to the curtained alcove where the four-poster bed stood. Magnolia sat beside her, patting her hand.

"Let's get you changed and into the bed," Hypatia said, offering the tailored navy silk pajamas that she favored. "Morgan, will you stay in case we need you?" If Simone should faint again, Hypatia wasn't sure that she and Magnolia together could get her into bed.

"I'll be just outside," Morgan said.

Hypatia and Magnolia helped Simone change from her jeans and T-shirt into the silk pajamas. The child was skin and bones. And scars. Magnolia clucked her tongue, but neither she nor Hypatia said a word. Hypatia's heart bled for what she saw, however, for what she knew the child had been through. She had to button the top for Simone, and it hung on her, much too large. Nevertheless, it would have to do.

After gently herding their new houseguest to the bed, Hypatia folded back the covers, and she and Magnolia aided as best they could while Simone laboriously climbed beneath the bedspread and top sheet.

"Thank you," she whispered, tears of sheer exhaustion standing in her eyes.

Impulsively, Hypatia bent and kissed Simone's ivory brow. She would spend much time in prayer for this one and, unless she missed her guess, for her nephew, too. Suddenly, she feared for Morgan. He'd lost one woman to another man and disease; Hypatia didn't want to see any part of that scenario played out in his life again. Straightening, she called out to him.

The door opened at once, and he came striding into the room. He bent over the bed, smoothing Simone's short hair. It struck Hypatia that she'd seen that unusual reddish-brown color before, but she couldn't think where or on whom.

"I can trust you to rest now, can't I?"

Simone sighed. "Yes."

"All right. Comfortable?"

"Very," Simone replied, stifling a yawn.

"Good. Now, stay there and sleep."

"Yes, sir, Professor Chatam, sir."

"I'll see you later."

Nodding, Simone closed her eyes and was asleep before they had tiptoed all the way across the sitting room to the door, but Hypatia waited until they were a good way along the landing before she asked, "Did you see it?"

"If you mean the scar just below her collarbone," Morgan replied grimly, "yes. She had a chemotherapy port."

"That would be my guess."

"And extensive abdominal surgery," Magnolia added softly.

Morgan sighed. "I knew something was wrong. From the way Brooks behaved, I'm guessing the cancer is behind her but that she hasn't fully recovered her strength yet."

"We'll see to it that she has the peace and quiet that she needs to recover," Hypatia promised.

They walked to the head of the stairs before he slipped his arms about each of their shoulders and said, "Have I mentioned lately that I thank God for my special aunties?"

Hypatia smiled fondly up at him. "Not lately."

"Well, I do," he told her with a squeeze. "Routinely. This world would be a much more difficult place without you. I'm especially thankful for you today. Simone needs a safe, quiet, comfortable haven right now."

"She has it," Magnolia told him.

"She has more than that," Hypatia added. "God is going to be hearing from us *routinely* about Miss Simone Guilland."

"I was counting on that," he told her with a smile.

"As you should. Now, will you stay to lunch?"

"I think I just might," he agreed, winking. "After all, you've got the best cook in town."

Hypatia smiled. Morgan was in and out of Chatam House all the time, and he often stayed for meals. Hypatia wondered if they'd be seeing him even more often now that Simone Guilland was in residence, however. She only hoped that it wouldn't lead to heartbreak. He'd already lost two women he'd loved to cancer—his stepmother and the woman he'd intended to marry. Surely God wouldn't raise that number.

Would He?

Chapter Four

An itch pulled her out of a dense fog and into a feeling of light. Only as she stirred in an effort to reach that place between her shoulder blades where the skin begged to be scratched did she come to realize that she was awakening from sleep. Rolling onto her back with a little noise of exasperation, she wiggled her shoulders to alleviate that bothersome niggle once and for all, only to find herself assailed with a fearful disorientation.

This was not her bed, not the too-hard mattress in the boardinghouse, not the thin, lumpy pad in the hospital, not even the cool, impersonal guest bed at the Guilland house in Baton Rouge. This was the warmest, softest, most comfortable bed she'd ever known. Simone sat up and opened her eyes in the same swift movement, and found the creams and gold and royal-blues of Chatam House all around her.

Memory came rushing back, how she had fainted

at the coffeehouse, been rushed to the emergency room in an ambulance, drugged by that nice Dr. Leland and then bullied into coming here by Morgan Chatam. She vaguely recalled her aunt bringing in a tea tray at some point and gobbling down those delicious ginger muffins that had been such a highlight of her childhood, and she vividly remembered being carried up the stairs by Morgan Chatam. College professors weren't supposed to be that strong and fit, that masculine. They were supposed to be bookish and stuffy and…not wildly attractive.

She flopped down onto the pillows with a huff. Her life wasn't going at all according to plan. When had it ever?

No matter. She felt fully recovered now. In fact, she felt wonderful. And ravenous. It was time to go home and back to work. Or possibly to class.

She looked around for a clock and found the backpack that she carried in lieu of a handbag on the nightstand next to the four-poster bed. Evidently, someone had fetched it from the coffeehouse. Reaching inside the partially unzipped front pocket, she pulled out her seldom-used cell phone and flicked the screen with her thumb. Six a.m. Oh, my. Apparently she had slept nearly around the clock. No wonder she was so hungry. A casual glance at the calendar icon brought her bolt upright in bed again.

Monday! Monday? How could it be Monday? That

would mean that she'd slept completely through Saturday *and* Sunday.

"You were more tired than you thought," said an amused voice.

Simone jerked to her right. At the same time, she grabbed for the covers, yanking them up around her throat. Hypatia Chatam smiled at her from the wing chair at her bedside. Garbed in a white silk dressing gown piped in navy and matching pajamas, she had caught her long, silver hair at the nape of her neck with a narrow white ribbon.

"My apologies. I didn't mean to frighten you. We were concerned because you slept so long and thought someone should sit with you."

Clapping a hand over her galloping heart, Simone huffed out a relieved breath. "I'm so sorry to have worried you."

"It's of no matter. You look much refreshed. I'll have your breakfast sent up. You can shower and dress whenever you like, and Chester will drive you over to the rooming house to pack your belongings."

"No!" Simone insisted automatically. The last thing she wanted was for her uncle to drive her around town. "That is, I—I should be going to class. Dr. Leland said particularly that I am able to attend school a-and master my studies."

Hypatia inclined her head. "In that case, I'll call Morgan."

Simone opened her mouth to protest but could think of no better option, so she closed it again.

"Your clothing has been laundered and put away," Hypatia informed her, rising from the chair. "You'll find toiletries in the bathroom. Is there anything else you need at the moment?"

Escape, Simone thought. She said, "No, thank you."

Nodding, Hypatia moved toward the foot of the bed. "As you've been working in a coffeehouse, I take it you drink the stuff."

"Yes, of course, but if you don't mind, I prefer tea this morning. My stomach's been empty too long, I think, for coffee."

Hypatia beamed at her. "I prefer tea every morning. It is more soothing, isn't it?"

"I think so," Simone said.

"I'm sure you would know," Hypatia told her kindly before turning away.

That comment seemed a little odd, but Simone put the thought aside for the moment. Slipping from the high bed, she padded on bare feet to the antique dresser, surprised to find her legs a little shaky. A few moments later, as she undressed to shower in the small but richly appointed bath, she glanced up into the mirror and saw the many scars that she bore on her too-thin body. She hazily recalled undressing in front of the Chatam sisters, and a little shiver of foreboding went through her. Her secrets, she feared, were no longer entirely her own.

Returning to the outer chamber minutes later, dressed and clean, she felt strong but starved. The sight of Hypatia fussing over a heavily laden round tray was welcome indeed. Simone gave her short hair a final rub before draping the towel over the back of the nearest chair. She plopped herself onto the seat and surveyed the contents of the tray in wonder. Fluffy scrambled eggs, crisp bacon, toast, fruit salad, apple juice, a pot of tea and two cups, butter, jelly and—unless her nose and memory deceived her—Aunt Hilda's famous ginger muffins, warm from the oven.

"I hope you didn't carry this upstairs yourself," she declared, quickly filling one of a pair of delicate china plates.

"No, no. We are blessed with a dumbwaiter just along the landing," Hypatia told her. "When you are done here, we'll send everything back downstairs, and anytime you want anything from the kitchen, all you have to do is call down." She pointed to the bedside table, where she had laid a paper with telephone numbers written on it. A sharp rap on the door had her bustling in that direction. "That will be Morgan," she said over her shoulder. "He was already on his way when I phoned."

As Simone realized for whom that second plate was intended, her stomach fluttered. She told herself that it was hunger, but she was not as good at lying to herself as she had used to be. Morgan came through the door wearing khakis and a collared knit shirt about the same color of rusty brown as his eyes. He carried a disposable cup of coffee in one hand and seemed as cheery and robust as it was possible to be before seven in the morning.

"Good morning, all." He bent to give his aunt a kiss on the cheek before nodding to Simone. "You look well rested."

She touched her damp hair self-consciously, murmuring, "I should."

He chuckled as his aunt reached for the extra teacup. "Since you brought coffee," she said, "I'll just help myself to some tea, if you don't mind."

"Please do," Simone replied.

At the same time, Morgan pulled out the other chair, saying, "Allow me."

Hypatia waved away the chair, chose a muffin and wandered toward the sofa, teacup and saucer in hand. "No, no, don't mind me. I'll just relax over here while the two of you enjoy your breakfast."

Morgan waited until she had lowered herself onto the couch, then he parked himself on the chair, rubbed his hands together enthusiastically and dove in. "Good thing I brought an appetite."

Simone gave him a noncommittal "um" and began to eat. The eggs were delicious.

"Sour cream," he said.

"What?"

"Hilda whips them with a dollop of sour cream," he explained, as if reading Simone's mind, "and parsley. I stole the recipe ages ago. At home, I add a touch of paprika and garlic powder." He winked, deepening his voice to add, "More manly that way."

Simone laughed. She couldn't help it. "Don't let Hilda hear you say that. She can't abide garlic powder." He straightened at that. Realizing what she'd let slip, she hastily added, "I imagine. Most *real* cooks can't."

He looked down at his plate. "Your family has cooks, do they?"

A heartbeat too late she said, "The Guillands keep three cooks, one for weekdays, which is four days a week, another for weekends, which is three days a week, and the third for special occasions." It wasn't a lie. The Guillands did have three cooks, and she hadn't said that they were her family. Not anymore, anyway.

"They sound prosperous."

She nodded, smiling slightly. He put down his fork, staring at her openly until she reached up a hand to smooth her hair again.

"You look fine," he told her, trying to read her mind again. "The short hair becomes you."

"Thank you. I—I sometimes think it makes me look too much like a child." She shook her head, wondering why she'd told him that. "I, ah, used to wear it long."

He looked down, picked up his fork again and said very casually, "Lost it to the chemotherapy, I suppose."

And there it was. Big secret number one exposed.

She gulped, made herself stay calm and waited until he looked at her. "Yes."

He sat back, touched a napkin to the corners of his mouth and asked, "Why didn't you want to tell me?"

"I was afraid the college would deny my admission application if it became known that I was recovering from cancer."

"But you're cancer free at this time, or so I assume."

"Yes, and I have been for nearly six months."

"But you're still weak and vulnerable."

She quietly said, "I've had a lot of upheaval in my life." Clamping her lips together, she looked him squarely in the eye. If he wanted anything else out of her, he'd have to pry it out with a crowbar and a scalpel. She'd said—and been through—enough. His cinnamon eyes plumbed hers for several seconds until finally he chuckled and shook his head.

"All right. Keep your own counsel. After breakfast, I'll drive you to class, and after class, I'll take you to the boardinghouse to pack your belongings."

"That isn't necessary," she said, shaking her head. "I'm fine now. You said yourself how well rested I look."

"And I intend for you to stay that way until you're fully recovered."

"But—"

"No buts, Simone," he told her firmly. "That's my price for keeping your health issues between us. You move in here until you are fully recovered, according to Dr. Leland and myself, or I go to the BCBC administration with a recommendation that your studies be delayed for at least a semester."

She gasped. "That's blackmail!"

"That's my considered judgment as your faculty adviser."

Curling her fists against the urge to throw something at his handsome head, she huffed out a calming breath, saying bitterly, "You leave me no choice."

"None at all," he admitted shamelessly. Sitting forward, he covered her hands with his much larger ones, saying, "Simone, I'm trying to help you."

Heat rolled up her arms, melting her fists into compliant little curls and filling her with an urgent need for…comfort, protection…something. That *something* felt alarmingly dangerous, like every mistake she'd ever made. She pulled her hands free, sitting back and folding her arms. Frowning, he blinked at her as if trying to decide what had just happened.

Picking up his fork again, he all but growled at her, "Eat your breakfast."

Her appetite had gone, but she cleaned her plate anyway. The sooner she regained her strength and put on some weight, the sooner she could get out of here. Hopefully that would happen before she stumbled across her sister. Perhaps, if she kept to her room here, she could avoid everyone who had any reason to know her.

Oh, Lord, let that be enough, she prayed desperately. *I just can't face Carissa now, not after everything that's happened. Please, just give me some time to get my strength back, at least. Then...then if she hates me, maybe I can bear it.*

Tears filled her eyes at the thought, but she willed them away, dug down deep for the strength that the hospital chaplain had told her was now hers and repeated silently one of the verses he had taught her from John 16.

"I have told you these things so that in Me you may have peace. In this world you will have trouble. But take heart! I have overcome the world."

Those words of Christ calmed her. She recalled how far she had come, off the streets and out of bad relationships, through life-threatening disease to earn a degree and press on for another. One day in the not-too-distant future, she would do something real and significant with her life to make up for all the pain, sorrow and foolishness of her past. Then maybe she could approach what was left of her family, confess all and show them that she could be trusted to take part in their lives once again. Then, maybe, Carissa could forgive her and they could be the kind of sisters they always should have been. But if not, Simone would have something to return to, something to give her life to, something worth laying at the feet of Christ when she joined her father in Heaven one day.

That was all she wanted now, and no handsome, overbearing, if well-meaning, college professor was going to get in her way.

Clearly, Morgan had misread Simone at their first meeting. She wasn't interested in him. Far from it. With every door that he opened for her, every hand of assistance that he offered, she gave a twitch of her chin that practically shouted, "Stay clear! Back away!"

He'd have happily obliged her if he could have, but for some reason he felt literally compelled to watch over her. Much thanks he received for his trouble. She grumbled and groused like the petulant child he was increasingly aware she was not.

"I don't see why I should take ski clothes to Chatam House."

"Why leave them here when you're not going to be staying here?"

The boardinghouse was even more shabby than Morgan recalled, but Simone's room was as neat as a pin, perhaps because most of her clothes were of the winter variety and remained packed away in boxes.

"Why do you have so many ski clothes anyway?" he asked. "I can't imagine that snow skiing is a big pastime around Baton Rouge." But then, she had done most of her undergraduate work in Colorado. He wondered if she would own up to it. She did and more.

"It is possible to travel outside of Louisiana, you know," she told him haughtily, "but as a matter of fact, I used to work on the ski slopes in Colorado. That's where I met my husband."

"Your husband!" Morgan yelped the words, feeling pricked and, oddly enough, betrayed.

She went pale as a sheet. "My ex-husband," she hurriedly amended, "or whatever you call him when the marriage is annulled."

Annulled! Morgan didn't think he'd ever heard of an annulled marriage in this day and age. The woman was a puzzle wrapped in a mystery inside of an enigma. She put trembling hands to her head and sighed.

"Oh, now look what you've gone and done." Dropping her hands, she stared at him accusingly. "There was no reason anyone had to know about that."

"There's nothing saying anyone does," he told her. Anyone *else,* that was. Folding his arms, he prepared to wait the rest of the day for the story, if necessary.

Recognizing his resolve, Simone stamped a foot. He thought for a moment that she would explode, but she glanced at the open door—a house policy, and a wise one—and instead sighed, throwing herself down to sit on the edge of the narrow bed. Morgan pulled out the desk chair and straddled it, folding his arms across the top edge of the back.

She made a face and said, "He's an only child from a wealthy family, used to getting his way, frankly, and...well, we had fun, so when he asked me to elope with him, I agreed. He told me up front that his parents, who were older, wouldn't approve but that they'd change their minds when we presented them with their first grandchild." She looked away, adding, "I actually thought I might be pregnant right away, but a routine physical exam turned up something else altogether."

"Cancer," Morgan surmised.

She nodded. "The doctors worked to save as much as they could, but..." She stilled herself and very calmly said, "I'll never have children."

The bravery behind that simple statement stabbed him to the heart, but he did his best not to show it.

"So, no hope of changing his parents' minds, then," he said lightly.

She sent him a wry, sad smile. "I'm not sure he even tried," she whispered huskily.

"Simone, I'm sorry," he told her, reaching out a hand. To his surprise, after only a brief hesitation, she warily slipped her hand into his. He squeezed her fingers, feeling the same flash of warmth that had taken him by surprise at the breakfast table. "I thank God that you eloped with him," he heard himself say.

She glanced up in obvious surprise. "Come again?"

"What he did was despicable," Morgan pointed out, "casting you off because of an illness, but if you hadn't married him, you might not have discovered the cancer until it was too late."

Her eyes widened, and her jaw slowly descended. "I never thought of it that way." Her gaze seemed to turn inward as she considered. "You're right, though. I had ignored certain symptoms for a long time, and I'd have gone right on ignoring them if I hadn't wanted to have a baby. I didn't see them as symptoms. They were normal to me."

"In a way, he did you a favor."

"Two, actually," she said drily. "First he married me. Then he unmarried me."

Morgan laughed. "I won't argue with that."

"The annulment was his parents' idea, of course."

"So he could avoid a settlement, no doubt."

"Oh, no, they were willing to pay handsomely to be rid of me. They paid for my schooling, every bit of it, past loans, current and future tuition."

"Ah." Morgan nodded. Now he understood that unusual tuition arrangement.

"Plus, they paid my hospital bills," Simone added. "In all honesty, I cannot fault their generosity."

"Only their sensitivity."

"Well, yes. I was served the annulment papers while I was still in the hospital after my last surgery."

Morgan flexed his shoulders, fighting an unfamiliar surge of anger. He didn't get angry. His was the cool head in the family. His older brother, Bayard, a banker, blustered and threw his considerable weight around as a matter of routine. His handsome younger brother, Chandler, had been a wild one, making his living in rodeo before his wife, Bethany, had tamed him. Morgan, the middle brother, had always been logical, laid-back and self-contained, channeling his baser emotions into the thrill of speed. He seldom felt more than irritation and never a sudden, almost blinding need to shake a certain someone until his teeth fell out. He tried to make sense of it.

"You'd think that at my age I wouldn't still be surprised by what goes on in this world."

She tilted her head, scolding him with, "You're hardly Methuselah."

It struck him just how old he'd begun to feel of late. And how he didn't feel that way with her. With other students, yes, but not with her. Just then he became aware of the scuffing of several feet in the doorway.

"Hey, Simone, where you been?" a male voice asked.

Only when she pulled free did Morgan realize that they still clasped hands. She sent a blinding smile to someone behind him.

"It turns out that I'm moving."

"Aw, that's too bad."

Aware suddenly of how this must look, Morgan rose and rolled the chair out of the way, saying, "Ms.

Guilland requires a room more conducive to study. As her faculty adviser, I was able to help her find a place." He turned, addressing those clumped together in the doorway. "How about some of you young guys carry down her boxes for her?"

They practically fell all over each other rushing to help. Even the girls hurried to fold bed linens and find boxes for what wasn't already packed. Morgan stood in the center of the chaos, trying to appear above it all, but painfully aware of the inquisitive, speculative glances that were tossed his way. And no wonder. BCBC had strict policies about faculty becoming involved romantically with students.

Of course, he and Simone were definitely *not* romantically involved, but just the appearance of such a thing was bad enough. What had possessed him to hold her hand like that? Even given all that she'd been through—and God knew the *woman* had been through enough—he ought to have better sense than to hold her hand like that, especially after what had happened at breakfast.

What had happened at breakfast, anyway?

He shook his head, not at all certain that he really wanted to know. Better just to leave it alone. Better just to leave *her* alone. He'd deposit her at Chatam House, where he knew she would be well cared for, and thereafter keep his distance. He'd done his duty as her faculty adviser. His aunties and Brooks could do the rest.

If he felt as though he might be abandoning her, well, that was nonsense. He wasn't her husband, after all.

For a moment, Morgan's blood boiled as he thought of her spoiled, insensitive ex serving her with annulment papers while she was recovering in the hospital from surgery, as if her value as a wife, a human being, had been diminished by her cancer. As if her entire reason for existing had been to give his parents grandchildren, as if she was nothing without a womb. As if she had not suffered enough loss already.

He'd seen the pain behind the mask of her serenity when she'd told him that she'd never be able to have children. Seen it, felt it and, for an instant, shared it. Even now he wanted to wrap his arms around her and promise her that the pain would fade, that everything would be all right, that she had more than enough to offer. Which was exactly why he wouldn't do any such thing.

All but running from the room, he went down to open the car, glad he'd brought the luxury sedan and not the two-seater. As it was, they couldn't fit everything inside, but he decided he'd send someone else for the rest of her things. After all, he had a reputation to defend, a career to protect. He told himself that it wasn't the temptation he feared so much as the speculation, the appearance of the thing, which was plenty of reason to keep his distance.

He found a couple of grad students willing to do

him a favor. Then, once he had her things unloaded at Chatam House, he told the aunts he had an appointment, which he did, and took off for an evening of unwinding at the racetrack.

Only as he blared around the oval on his motorcycle, a black-on-white blur, thanks to his protective, one-piece leather suit, did he recall that he still had to arrange a ministry assignment for her. Well, that shouldn't be too difficult, given his connections and her field of study. On the other hand, nothing had proven easy with Simone Guilland so far, nothing except looking at her, touching her…nothing except getting in over his head.

Chapter Five

For the third time that morning, Simone looked up to find Chester staring at her via the rearview mirror of the Chatam sisters' long sedan, or so it seemed. It could have been her imagination. He'd said nothing beyond a polite "Good morning" when he'd opened the car door for her at Chatam House earlier on that Thursday. As the elegant town car had moved over the gracefully shaded streets toward the college, however, he'd seemed to be keeping an eye on her.

She tried not to squirm, not to let her heart race with the fear of discovery, but she couldn't help wishing that Morgan had come to take her to her classes again, even though she'd vowed to keep her distance from the handsome professor. She hadn't seen him since Monday, except in the lecture hall on Wednesday. He'd come to class in a black leather jacket and jeans, carrying a motorcycle helmet, his hair looking rumpled and windblown. The girl next to Simone had whispered that Professor Chatam was hot. Simone had pretended not to hear her, but a tiny part of her wondered if she was playing second fiddle to a motorbike. Was she subjected to Chester's too-curious stares because Morgan preferred riding his motorcycle to giving her a lift?

It was a depressing thought and patently absurd. She had no claim on Morgan Chatam's attention. Even if having her uncle drive her to and from the campus was unnerving.

Pushing Morgan from her mind, she concentrated on what mattered most. If her full identity became known, her family might enter a state of shock for a time, but they'd quickly begin to ask questions—and dislike the answers. Eventually, most likely sooner rather than later, they'd turn her out. She, after all, had abandoned them first, running away to live her own life, so sure that she knew best and could do better without them.

How she had resented them all! Her selfish, self-centered mother had blown apart their family with her quest for "fulfillment" and "appreciation." Her unassuming, plodding father had stubbornly refused to be more, have more, provide more. After years of struggle, Alexandra, her mother, had wanted excitement and excess, while Marshall, her father, had wanted contentment and simplicity. They were each so entrenched in their positions that they had never even considered meeting somewhere in the middle. Worse, each had been determined to win their daughters to a particular viewpoint. Carissa had escaped into an early marriage, leaving her baby sister trapped between them in a tug-of-war that seemed both endless and pointless. Oh, how Simone had resented Carissa for that!

Well, she'd showed them. She'd gotten out of the middle, finally—and into one rotten mess after another. Every time she'd told herself that she'd go home as soon as she fixed things, but something or someone always got in the way, and before she'd known it, she'd been too ashamed to show her face in Texas again. She'd tried to do better, to make something of herself. When she'd met Aaron Guilland, she'd thought he was her ticket back into the bosom of her family. She'd envisioned herself returning home, a well-dressed wife and mother, a member of the Baton Rouge upper echelon. She'd imagined that both of her parents and Carissa would be pleasantly surprised, and that eventually all of her sins would be forgiven. What largesse she had planned to shower on them! Instead, she'd spent eighteen months fighting cancer and making her peace with God while gathering the courage to return home alone, broken, humbled, a shadow of her former self. And too late.

Her father might have welcomed her, but he was gone. In all likelihood, her mother would only mock her. Her sister could only resent her. No, Simone told herself, she had nothing to offer but too much of the wrong kind of experience, a mountain of regret and a tale of woe. She looked away from her uncle's curious, unknowing gaze and stared blindly out the window.

"Would you like me to drop you at the administration building again today, miss?"

"That will be fine."

Within moments, he had pulled the car to the curb. As she got out, her backpack slung over one shoulder, he asked, "What time would you like to be picked up?"

"I wouldn't," she said automatically, quickly adding, "That is, it's not necessary."

He twisted in his seat, his face puckered in concern. "Are you sure? The Chatams wouldn't like you to walk."

"No, no, I won't." She hoped. Surely she could find someone to give her a ride. She did have a few friends, and it wasn't far. She just didn't think she could bear another ride in the car with Chester today. If worst came to worst, she'd call a taxi. "Thank you."

"My pleasure, miss."

She said a swift prayer as she walked to her first class, and by the end of the day, she'd arranged a ride home and transportation for Friday. She'd even agreed to join some friends for breakfast at the coffee shop on Saturday morning, which would give her a chance to pick up her last paycheck and get out of Chatam House on a day when she didn't have classes.

It felt good, after keeping to her room all Friday afternoon and evening, to go out with friends on Saturday morning and talk of nothing more pressing than assignments and projects. Simone felt older than the other single graduate students, two girls and a guy from the old boardinghouse, but she didn't let that stop her from hopping into a rattletrap car with them and heading down to the coffeehouse for muffins and lattes. Everyone was curious about her living arrangements, but she fobbed them off by saying that her arrangement with the Chatam sisters, who were well known for their support of Buffalo Creek Bible College, was only temporary.

As they drew near the door of the coffee shop, she noticed a green-and-white moped chained to a light pole out front. A big For Sale sign had been taped to the handlebars, and a neat little helmet had been parked upon the seat. When she stopped to look, so did her friends. A fellow sitting at one of the sidewalk tables noticed and came over to make a sales pitch. The moped had belonged to him and then his son, but the boy had recently bought his first car and was selling the "old 'ped" to raise money for new rims. Her guy friend knew more about such things than she did, and he asked some intelligent questions, eliciting useful information, including a cash price that seemed more than reasonable to Simone.

After a few minutes, their group wandered on inside to place their orders. Simone received her paycheck. The proprietor apologized because he couldn't hold Simone's job for her, but she was surprised and pleased to find that the check was more than she'd expected—more than enough, in fact, to buy that moped and possibly put an end to her transportation quandaries once and for all. She chewed her bottom lip, uncertain.

Motorbikes could be dangerous, but a moped wasn't a real motorcycle. The man had said that it had a top speed of thirty miles per hour. Yet it was perfectly legal to ride on city streets, the same as a bicycle. She'd need a permit, a license and insurance, of course, but he'd said all were easy and inexpensive to obtain, especially for an adult. Her friends could see that she was seriously considering it.

"Do you want to pray about it?" one of them asked.

Simone smiled. That was the great thing about attending a Christian college. No one would have dared ask her that question at her old school. "I would, yes."

They all linked hands and bowed their heads. After a moment, Simone realized that they were waiting for her to speak the prayer.

She stumbled uncertainly through it, then looked up to find the gentleman with the moped coming through the door. He held a cell phone to his ear and was speaking to someone on the other end.

"I'll see," he said, walking up next to her. "Miss," he said, "if you're interested, we could come down on the price maybe twenty-five dollars and throw in the helmet and security chain with the deal."

Simone blinked and smiled at her friends. "That sounds like confirmation to me." She nodded at the man. "I'll take it."

He spoke into the phone again. "Go ahead, son. Make the deal on the rims." Pocketing the phone, he smiled at Simone and said, "You've just made a sixteen-year-old very happy."

She laughed, and they agreed to meet at the local Department of Motor Vehicles office the following Tuesday morning to complete the deal.

On Tuesday afternoon, after easily acquiring her driving permit, she puttered onto campus on her moped a little saddened that God had made it possible for her to minimize contact with her aunt and uncle while living at Chatam House. Obviously, she was not meant to reveal herself to her family, at least not yet. Strangely, that did not bother her as much as had Morgan barely seeming to register her presence in class that week.

By the time the weekend rolled around, she was feeling almost invisible. Then the Chatams made it plain that they expected her to attend church on Sunday. She was nervous about going until one of them mentioned that their nephew Phillip, Carissa's husband, was the only local Chatam who did *not* attend the Downtown Bible Church. Instead, he and his family attended Buffalo Creek Christian Church with Chester and Hilda.

Relieved, Simone happily went along and enjoyed the service. Morgan, however, was not in attendance. She did meet his father, Hub, though, a sweet older gentleman. He said something about Morgan visiting his younger brother for the weekend.

"Just an excuse to ride his motorcycle on the open road, most likely," said Morgan's brother-in-law, Stephen. Kaylie, Stephen's wife and Morgan's sister, made a face.

"Oh, as if you wouldn't jump at the chance if I'd let you." She winked at Simone, adding, "Hockey isn't dangerous enough for him." Patting her rounded middle, she confided, "I want my baby's father in one large piece, thank you very much."

Simone smiled around the pain blossoming in her chest. Morgan hadn't mentioned that his sister and her husband were expecting, but then he wouldn't, knowing what he did about her. Obviously, he hadn't told anyone else about her problem, or at least not very many people. She had hoped he wouldn't. It was too personal a secret, too poignant a loss to share with just anyone.

Perhaps it was silly of her, but she couldn't help feeling a little glad that she could trust him with her secrets. He hadn't told the university about her cancer, after all, and he hadn't spread it around that she was half a woman, unable to bear children and so unfit for marriage that the man who had professed to love her, the man she'd thought to be her ticket back into her family's good graces, had annulled their marriage while she was still in the hospital recovering from the surgery that had taken any chance of motherhood from her.

Yes, it was nice to be able to trust Morgan with her secrets, some of them, anyway. It was nice everything seemed to be working out.

If only it didn't all hurt so much.

Mentally congratulating himself on his nonchalance, Morgan hailed Simone after class on the next to last Monday in September. He'd managed to keep away from her for nearly two whole weeks, though he had picked up the phone countless times, only to put it down again without dialing, and had talked himself out of dropping by Chatam House on a daily basis.

"Do you have a minute? I need to speak to you about a ministry assignment."

She gave him a taut smile and spoke in that husky voice that seemed to dance across his nerve endings. "Of course." Stepping out of the queue that filed through the door, she slipped her backpack from her shoulders and let it drop to the floor.

He parked himself on the corner of the desk in the lecture hall and took stock. She seemed none the worse for wear. She'd put on weight, her face had gained a bit of color and her hair had grown enough to lie down, framing her big gray eyes with delicate wisps and the faintest bit of curl. She looked achingly lovely. He couldn't help noticing that she had the most delicate ears he'd ever seen on a grown woman.

Clearing his throat, he glanced down at the pencil in his hand. "I've given it some thought, and considering your major and your interests, I wonder if you would like to work with my father in one of DBC's new ministries. Let me explain."

He went on to detail the Downtown Bible Church program for youth and young adults that his father had spearheaded. Those involved ran the gamut from teens without adequate supervision and guidance to a few who literally lived on the street. The latter they mostly moved into the foster system or group homes as soon as they confirmed the situation. Some, however, were too old for foster care, so they were transitioned into adult homeless shelters.

"The ministry isn't licensed to house anyone, you understand, except on a short-term emergency basis, but it does try to match resources with needs, and it gives them a safe place to go for much of the day and some of the evening."

"Sounds interesting," Simone said. "Knowing your father, I assume that he's easy to work with."

Surprised, Morgan grinned at her. "You know my dad?"

"I met Pastor Hub at church. Your aunts introduced us."

"Of course."

If he'd been there, he'd have known that, but he'd thought it best to keep out of her way by running off to visit his kid brother. Chandler and Bethany were doing very well on their horse ranch in Stephenville. Their little boy was still a toddler, but he was absolutely fearless on horseback, just like his dad. They were talking about having another child, but Morgan wouldn't share that bit of news with Simone for anything. He'd thought of her when the subject had come up, and his heart had ached for her.

He wondered suddenly if she'd met his sister, Kaylie. She and Stephen were expecting their first. His heart in his throat, he fixed his mind on the matter at hand.

"Well, should I tell Dad you're interested?"

"Yes, please."

"Excellent. I'll fix it with him and drive you over there, say, tomorrow evening."

"Oh, that won't be necessary," she said, bending down to snag the straps of her backpack and haul it up into her arms. "I have transportation now. I'll be fine." With that, she reached into the top of the pack and withdrew a simple little pot-style scooter helmet.

Morgan came off the desk in a flying leap and snatched the thing out of her hands. It didn't weigh eight ounces, barely enough to protect her skull. Horror flashed through him.

"You're riding a cycle?"

"Just a moped," she said with a chuckle. "A little old ancient thing hardly bigger than a bicycle."

Morgan nearly swallowed his tongue. "What? That's insane! You'd be better off on a bicycle. No, wait. You're not strong enough for a bicycle. What are you thinking?"

She tossed her backpack to the floor again and glared at him, her hands at her hips. "I'm thinking that it's none of your business."

"None of my—" Aware that he'd raised his voice, he broke off in midsentence and closed his eyes, slowly counting to ten. "Motorized two-wheeled vehicles are dangerous," he said, quite reasonably.

"You ride one," she pointed out, most rudely, he thought.

"I am an expert. I race the things. I am certainly qualified to ride them on city streets."

Sticking out her chin, she said mulishly, "So am I. I have a permit and everything."

"That's beside the point! You're still recovering. You're—" she glanced around them wildly, but they were quite alone now "—still weak," he went on doggedly.

"I don't even have to pedal," she pointed out, reaching for the helmet.

He set it on the desk behind him, out of her reach. Shaking his head, he said, "I have to speak to Brooks about this."

She folded her arms. "You are the most arrogant, heavy-handed, presumptuous—"

"Faculty adviser," he reminded her. He didn't need her to tell him that he was overstepping his bounds, but given the circumstances, he just didn't see what else he could do. The thought of her riding off on that tiny *death trap* gave him the shudders. If this was what came from keeping his distance, well, he'd just have to do better. "I'll drive you home," he stated flatly, leaving no room for argument. Nevertheless, he thought he might well be in for a fight.

For several long seconds, she glared at him, holding herself so rigidly that he expected to see steam start leaking from her ears at any moment. Finally, she turned and marched to the door, leaving him to retrieve the backpack and bring it along.

A smile caught Morgan as he bent to snag the straps of the backpack. He didn't know why, really. The woman was as frail as eggshells, but she'd been out zipping around town on a moped that couldn't get out of the way of a paper bag blowing in the wind, her only protection a pathetic little helmet that might have saved her from a minor concussion but nothing more. Still, she had gumption. She'd found herself some transportation—inadequate, but transportation—and she didn't like being told what to do one little bit. But he couldn't let her go chugging off on her own, especially not after he hefted that backpack. The thing was heavy, too heavy for her to be lugging around by herself and certainly too heavy for her to be hauling about on "a little old ancient" moped. It was a wonder she hadn't fallen over on the thing already. As he couldn't very well go schlepping around campus after her, toting her books like some lovesick swain, and drive her everywhere she needed to go, he'd have to get her a wheeled tote and provide her with proper transportation somehow. Obviously Chester had other things to do besides drive her around; either that or Simone couldn't bring herself to impose on him and the aunties when she needed to go somewhere. Well, they'd see about that.

"What about my moped?" she grumbled as they walked to his car.

"Give me the key. I'll have someone drive it over to Chatam House and park it," he said.

"And then what?"

"We'll decide that later." *After* he had spoken to Brooks about her. One way or another, he was going to get an accounting of her physical condition.

She didn't utter a word all the way to Chatam House. She didn't even look at him, and she didn't wait for him to come around the car and open the door for her, either. Instead, she bailed out of the Beemer the instant it stopped and reached back in to pull out the backpack before he could get to her.

"Here," he said, reaching for the thing, "I'll carry that in for you."

"No, thank you," she retorted snippily, swinging it up onto her shoulder. "I can manage."

Morgan resisted the urge to grind his teeth. "Simone, I'm just trying to—"

"Yes, yes, trying to help and all that," she said, moving up the walkway. She muttered something about "petty tyrants" and marched up the steps to the porch.

Morgan considered going after her, glanced at his wristwatch and decided against it. Let her stew, if that made her happy. He was going to catch Brooks before he made midmorning rounds. She slammed the front door of Chatam House just as Morgan dropped back down behind the steering wheel of his beloved BMW Z4.

He let off some steam getting to the doctor's office across the street from the hospital. It was a short trip from Chatam House made all the shorter by his venting of his irritation. His timing proved impeccable. Brooks came out of the side door marked Private just as Morgan pulled the rumbling Beemer into the reserved space that he always claimed as his own.

Brooks shoved his hands into the pockets of his white coat and grinned. "To what do I owe the honor of this ambush?" he asked as Morgan climbed out of the car.

"To one very stubborn graduate student."

"What has Ms. Guilland done now?"

"She's riding a moped."

Brooks gave him a bland look. "And?"

"And I'm worried that she isn't strong enough. She's carting around a backpack that weighs almost as much as she does and wearing a little soup pot of a helmet that wouldn't protect the brain box of a gerbil."

"Well, what do you want me to do about it?"

"I want you to tell her to cut it out. That she's not healthy enough for riding around on a two-wheeled motorized vehicle. Or tell me that so I can tell her. I am her faculty adviser, and…" The grin that Brooks tried to hide behind a raised hand and a bowed head set Morgan off. "What? I *am* her faculty adviser, and she *has* had cancer."

"So she told you, did she?"

"I guessed. She confirmed it. What I don't know," he went on, trying not to fidget, "is how likely it is to come back."

Brooks got that mulish look he always got when a patient's confidentiality was at risk, but Morgan waited, not even daring to breathe, and just when he was at the point of prayer, pleading or pounding, Brooks caved.

"Not very. I got her records, and from what I can tell, they took all the affected organs."

Morgan nodded, saying softly, "She told me what that cost her."

"The treatment was very aggressive, but it had to

be. In time, she'll regain her strength and be fine, I think."

"But she'll never have children."

"No. She'll never have children."

"She wanted to."

"Yes, I know. It's in the records."

"Should she be riding a moped?"

Brooks shrugged. "I don't know, Morgan. Bring her to see me, if you're so concerned, and I'll make an evaluation then."

"What about driving a car?"

"Has she been passing out?"

Morgan considered and shook his head. "No. Someone would have called me."

"Well, then, provided she has a license, I don't see why not."

Rubbing his chin, Morgan weighed the options. "Maybe I should get her a car." To his chagrin, Brooks burst out laughing. "Now what's your problem? I just don't want the girl to kill herself getting to school. I am—"

"Her faculty adviser. Sure. And her self-appointed white knight all rolled into one, apparently."

Morgan felt heat rise in his throat and face, but he tried to brazen it out. "Oh, come on. She's a student."

"And beautiful and brave and wounded."

He tried not to, but Morgan couldn't help bristling. Of course she was beautiful. And brave. And wounded. When he thought of all she'd been through, he ached for her, but here she was starting a new life for herself when so many others would have curled into a ball and tried to make the world go away. Naturally Brooks would notice those things, but Morgan didn't want him to. Especially Brooks. His friend. The man who had married the woman Morgan had loved, the woman they had both loved.

This was not, however, history repeating itself. This was duty. Morgan knew that because he had prayed that it be so. He had prayed for the purest of motives where Simone Guilland was concerned, and he trusted that God would give him nothing less.

Anytime now.

Chapter Six

"It's a wonderful facility," Simone gushed.

Morgan had driven her over to the Youth and Young Adult Ministry Center after prayer meeting at Downtown Bible Church that Wednesday evening, where she and his father had greeted each other like old friends. Now they talked as if they were already colleagues, ignoring Morgan as though he wasn't even there. He didn't like that very much.

Hub smiled. "Amazing what you can do with an old warehouse, isn't it? My grandfather built this place to hold cotton bales. He made his fortune shipping cotton on the railroad."

"And now you've put it to use for kids who are riding the rails," Simone surmised.

"We get a few of those," Hub said. "Most go on to the big rail yards in Dallas or Fort Worth, but the more timid ones hop off here. I think it seems safer to them." His gaze turned inward. "I never realized, never even thought about it."

"Most folks don't," Simone told him, "unless they've been homeless."

"I suppose that's true," Hub replied. "One of our board members at DBC is the yard manager for the railroad here, though, and he brought this need to our attention. We were surprised to find that we have more at-risk young people than we knew right here in town. This place has become a safe haven for them."

"What's the age range?"

"Thirteen to twenty, but we try to keep them seg-regated into groups below and above seventeen, the legal age of emancipation."

"There are overnight facilities?"

"Emergency only. We call Child Protective Ser-vices if the youngster is under seventeen years old. Occasionally they don't have a placement, so they send a worker to stay here with the child until some-thing comes open. It's usually only one night. If they're seventeen or older, they have to go to the adult homeless shelter, but they can come back here during the day. We offer them food, recreation, lit-eracy and GED classes, as well as counseling and someplace to bathe and wash their clothes. We also try to connect them with social and employment ser-vices. For the local kids, we're sort of a safe hangout. For the homeless ones…"

"You don't have to tell me," Simone proclaimed. "I've been there. For those homeless kids, this place is the answer to a prayer."

Shocked, Morgan wondered how a girl from a family with three chefs on the payroll had wound up homeless, even for a short time. No, wait, that was the Guilland family—her ex's family. Frowning, Morgan realized that Simone had actually told him very little about her own personal background. He knew that she'd worked on the ski slopes in Colorado and attended classes at a college there, but beyond that he knew only about her illness and her disastrous attempt at marriage. Perhaps it was best that he didn't know. The more he knew about her, the more he liked her.

Hub said something about her heart being in ministry to homeless youth.

"I suppose that's true," Simone admitted, smiling.

"Perhaps that was God's purpose in your own experience," Hub went on.

"Do you think so?" she asked wistfully. "I'd like to think it had a purpose."

"It must certainly account for your maturity," Hub said.

"Oh, I don't know about that." She shook her head, sighing. "Sometimes I amaze myself with my own stupidity."

Hub chuckled. "The first sign of wisdom."

She laughed. "Well, there's hope for me, then."

After a few more minutes of discussion, they agreed that she would work fifteen to twenty hours per week. The stipend was small, but she wasn't pay-ing rent, and Hub made no bones about wanting to turn the whole organization over to someone else capable of handling it at the first opportunity.

"I'm not getting any younger, you know," he said.

They shook hands on it, and she was hired. When Morgan stepped up and announced he'd walk her through the building while Hub closed up the place, she seemed surprised to find him there. That pricked his male vanity, which was probably a good thing, or so he told himself.

"That went well," Morgan assessed, strolling along beside her.

"I think so. But I don't buy that 'I'm not getting any younger' guff. How old is he, anyway?"

"Seventy-nine as of this past August."

"Wow. He has more energy than I do."

"He hasn't been ill."

"I hope he never is."

Morgan nodded in agreement with that. Hub had buried two wives, and for a time he had convinced himself that he was feeble, but he'd snapped out of it when Morgan's sister, Kaylie, had married.

"The Chatams are known for their heartiness," Morgan told her. "My grandpa died at ninety-two, and his father was even older. And, as Brooks is fond of pointing out, those were the days before medicine had made much of itself."

She smiled. "Praise God for modern medicine, is what I say."

"Amen."

They exited the building with its old-fashioned brick facade and went down a trio of concrete steps to the dusty parking spot below. He let her in the passenger door of the BMW and went around to get behind the wheel.

"I'm glad Dad's so spry," he said conversationally, "because I've always figured I'd be the one to take care of him in his old age."

"Oh? Why you?"

He started up the engine, engaged the gears and backed out of the parking space. "My brothers and sister are all married and either have families or are starting families, but I've just got me, so it only seems logical that I be the one to look after Dad when he can no longer look after himself." He put the transmission in gear, moving the car forward. "I think he thought Kaylie would do it. In fact, I don't think he wanted her to get married at all." He paused the car at the edge of the lot before pulling out onto the street. "She can thank our dear aunties for that. They didn't marry. Instead, they took care of their father until he died. At ninety-two."

"But Odelia and Kent—"

"Have been married just over a year," he said, shifting gears.

Simone gaped at him. "That's all?"

"It was a year in July. Oh, they were engaged way

back when, but they broke up for some reason. And got back together fifty years later."

"What a story!"

He chuckled. "It's the family love story."

"What about you?" Simone asked. "Why haven't you married?"

He slowed at a dip in an intersection, downshifting. "I wanted to marry." He surprised himself by adding, "She married Brooks Leland instead."

Simone caught her breath, but it might have been the way he accelerated.

After a moment, she asked, "What happened?"

"I don't really know. I asked her to marry me. She said yes. We were planning a wedding. Then a couple months before the big day, she gave me back the ring. The next thing I knew, she married my best friend."

"That's awful."

It seemed odd that he could smile about it now, but he did just that. "I certainly thought so at the time."

"No wonder you don't like Dr. Leland."

Morgan shot Simone a surprised look. "I love Brooks," he blurted unashamedly. "Brooks Leland is my best friend."

"But—"

"I hated him at the time, it's true, and I went off on a real tear for a while." He focused his attention on the scene unfolding outside his windshield, even as the words reeled off his tongue. "Wine, women and *stupidity*. But before long I started to hate me even more than I hated him, so I got myself right with God and went on with my life." He slowed and made a turn before saying, "Then, a year or so after they married, I realized that Brigitte was ill."

"What was it?" Simone asked softly.

He didn't know why he whispered it. "Inoperable brain tumor." He made himself go on. "She had some good months still, but she died just over two years after they married." To his surprise, Simone reached over and covered his hand on the gearshift knob with her own.

"I'm so sorry."

"We had enough time to make our peace," he said, "and I got back two people I loved, even if it wasn't the way I'd imagined."

"You've never felt that God punished them for what they did to you?"

Shocked, he took his eyes off the road long enough to gape at her. "No, never." He couldn't help wondering what had prompted such a question. "I think it was all for the best. She said to me once that if her illness had happened while she was with me, I'd have made her fight it. And she was right. I couldn't have done what Brooks did. He looked at the medical options, realized that he'd be putting her through a lot of pain and misery for no good reason other than his own desire to hold her here, so he let her go. That was what she wanted, to live her life to the fullest while she had it, not to live sicker than she had to."

"Sometimes," Simone said slowly, "the cure really is worse than the disease."

"I know that's true," Morgan told her, "but I don't know how you...don't fight."

"There was a moment," Simone said, "when I thought about giving up."

"You must have weighed the cost and wondered if it was worth it."

"That's it exactly."

"But you fought." He turned his hand palm up so he could squeeze her hand. "Brigitte was only twenty-five, so about your age, and it was nearly sixteen years ago. Medicine is light-years ahead of where they were then, but I'm not sure if, even now, she would choose to fight her disease."

"It's not always an easy decision."

"I understand that. I'm just saying that, for me, in the end..."

"You would have to fight, no matter how small the odds."

"Yes. Even if it might not be the right thing to do."

"So Brooks was the right man for her."

"Yes."

"I'm glad you have that assurance."

"So am I. And I'm glad that you chose to fight your disease, no matter the cost."

She smiled, nodded and took her hand away, changing the subject. "So why haven't you married? It's been sixteen years!"

He shrugged, chuckling. "I don't know. I was always open to it, but it just didn't happen. Now, at forty-five, I'm too old for it, too set in my ways."

"Now, that's just sad," Simone chided. "You could still be a father, after all."

He shook his head. "I'm not sure I'd want to start all that at this late date."

"But you said yourself that the Chatams are a hearty, long-lived bunch."

"I like my life just as it is, thank you very much, and this world has plenty of Chatams already."

"Please yourself, then, Professor."

"I always do," he admitted, grinning.

When, he wondered, his grin feeling strained, had that started to seem just a bit lonely?

Hub joked that she didn't let the air settle before she was off on a new project, but Simone knew too well how desperate a kid on the street could feel. Having someplace to go, even for a little while, when night closed in, would be a real comfort. Hub agreed to the idea of an evening "check-in" for homeless teens in the area, provided two adults were always on hand. Morgan promised to round up graduate students to staff two-hour shifts.

Half a dozen kids showed up that first evening. One eighteen-year-old, Rina, was overweight and sloppy with short blond hair, a sullen attitude and an eyebrow ring. She walked out in a huff when Simone suggested she find a job, but the girl seemed entirely capable of supporting herself, just unwilling.

Hub declared himself thrilled with Simone's efforts, and Morgan seemed pleased with the reports he received. Simone felt that she was doing something worthwhile, something that counted.

She'd have been happy if not for Chester. She did her best to stay out of her uncle's way, but whenever she came across him, Chester always looked at her as if he was trying to puzzle out something about her.

She had quietly resumed riding her moped after it had been returned to the estate, taking care to park where she wasn't likely to be seen and leaving the helmet with the bike. No one had told her not to ride the thing, after all—no one but Morgan, and he had no true authority over her.

To raise extra cash, she started selling her ski gear online, which allowed her to throw a little money at the homeless kids who most needed it. When the storm clouds rolled in during that second week in October, she thought about dipping into her savings to take a taxi over to the mission, but in the end, she couldn't bring herself to spend her funds that way. Instead, she donned a bright orange hooded plastic poncho over her helmet and climbed on her trusty moped that Thursday evening. The poncho was one she'd used on the ski slopes when wet, slushy snow had made navigation miserable. She tucked the ends up under her and used plastic sleeves, called gaiters, to protect her lower legs from splashes. Then she headed across town.

What had started as a steady drizzle soon became a drenching downpour, however. By the time she puttered into the rutted parking lot, she could barely see the street in front of her headlamp, and her pant legs were soaked from the knee to midcalf. She parked right next to the steps and scrambled up them blindly, lunging for the door beneath a veritable waterfall of runoff. As the heavy metal door closed behind her with a decided *ka-shunk,* she swept off the poncho, trying to minimize the rain spatter on the slick concrete floor of the corridor, and reached for the chin strap of her helmet, only to freeze at the sound of an all-too-familiar voice.

"I don't believe it! What on earth were you thinking, riding that thing over here?"

Simone mentally sighed. "Hello to you, too, Morgan."

"I mean it, Simone. Of all the stupid, illogical things to do!"

"I'm fine."

"You're not fine. You're soaked. Your jeans are wet."

"Four inches of my jeans are wet," she pointed out, pushing past him to carry the dripping poncho and helmet down the hall.

"Your shoes are wet," he said accusingly, and so they were. The rubber soles squeaked on the concrete.

"I'll take them off."

"And go barefoot on cold concrete?"

"It won't kill me."

"It might."

She wasn't going to argue that point with him. Instead, she turned, sighed and conceded. "All right. It was foolish of me to ride the moped over here in the rain. I should've taken a taxi."

"You should have had Chester drive you."

"No," she said before she could think better of it.

"Why not?"

"Doesn't matter. I shouldn't have ridden the moped in the rain."

"You're never going to let Chester drive you, are you?" Morgan demanded, folding his arms. He seemed to take up a lot of room there in the narrow corridor.

She tried to think of a safe, plausible answer, and when she couldn't come up with one, she simply turned on her heel and walked away, flipping on light switches as she went. Pausing at the double swinging door to the large, gymnasium-style meeting room, she fixed him with a curious gaze, and asked, "What are you doing here, Morgan?"

"I couldn't get anyone else to come out on a night like this, and I knew you were going to need help."

As if to prove that statement, the door opened and two boys stumbled in. Both were drenched and looked to be in their late teens.

"Nasty night," one of them said.

"I'll get some towels," Morgan muttered. "Wait there."

Before he got back, there were two more. Simone would get one placed and another would show up, and so it went until they locked the door. Rina, the chunky blonde with the eyebrow ring and oversize clothes, arrived just as Morgan returned with a small pickup truck and a trailer. She had obviously been crying, but her clothes and hair were dry, so she'd been in out of the rain. Simone was too busy trying to figure out how she could help the girl to bother about Morgan rolling the moped up onto the trailer.

"Do you need a place to stay?"

"Naw," Rina said, "I was just bored. Thought I'd see if there was anybody around."

"Do you need a ride somewhere?"

The girl shook her head, her gaze darting away. She waved a hand at the moped, asking, "What're you doing with that?"

"Taking it to storage in my garage," Morgan answered, prompting Simone to scowl.

"I didn't agree to that."

"It's late," he said. "We can argue later."

Rina snickered. "Y'all sound like my folks."

Simone rolled her eyes, hoping no one noticed the flush of color across her cheeks. How could anyone mistake her and Morgan Chatam for a couple? Oddly enough, though, it sometimes felt that way.

* * *

"This pickup is yours?" she asked as they bounced across the rutted parking lot.

"Yep." Morgan grinned. He'd had this conversation repeatedly over the years.

"Just how many vehicles do you have?"

"Several."

"How many do you need?"

"Several."

"Whatever for?"

"Various reasons."

"Such as?"

"Sometimes you need to haul something, and sometimes you need to race something, and sometimes you just need to drive something slick and fast. Other times you need to haul around a whole carload of people in comfort."

"You *need* to race and drive something slick and fast?" she asked drily.

"*I* do," he told her unrepentantly.

She rolled her eyes, which made him grin.

"You know, of course, how absurd that sounds," she said.

"I know that what I drive is my business," he told her, "and has been for a good many years."

She drew two fingers across her lips, turned them as if turning a key in a lock and flipped them as if throwing away the key. Morgan laughed.

"Good girl. You'll give me no argument then when I add the moped to my collection."

She opened her mouth to do just that, but he wagged a finger at her. "Uh-uh-uh. Your health comes first. Okay?"

She took a deep breath, frowned and said nothing. Morgan smiled grimly. He should have done this right at the beginning, but he kept trying to keep his distance. He couldn't have her riding mopeds in rainstorms, though. Both of them needed their heads examined.

He drove to his home. The sturdy, graceful redbrick house with its stone chimneys and arched doorways had been built in 1928. He loved the clay tile roof and multipaned windows, as well as the terracotta floors and paneled walls inside. It had no garage, just a two-bay carport on one end. He drove straight through the second bay, past the Beemer and on down the lane to the building at the back of the property, which was less garage than warehouse. He punched the automatic door opener attached to the visor and waited for the second of three doors to rise.

Her jaw dropped as he pulled into the clean, tidy, well-lit space.

"Oh. My. Word."

"We all have our vices," he told her. "I don't just like to own vehicles, I like to tinker with them."

"My dad would have loved this," she said, looking around. "He was a tinkerer. He'd work on any old motor, even a lawn mower."

"Was?" Morgan echoed.

Her smile faded. "Yes. Deceased."

"Was it sudden?" Morgan asked kindly.

"No," she answered. "He was ill a long time." She opened the truck door and got out then.

Well, if she was going to keep secrets, she couldn't blame him for trying to uncover them. He got out and walked over to the little silver coupe parked in the far left bay.

"Come over here," he said, "and let me see your driver's license."

She reached into the truck for her backpack and dug out her wallet. After she carried it over to him, he photographed her driver's license and opened an app on his smartphone.

"What are you doing?"

"Adding you to my insurance."

"What?"

He looked at her over the edge of the phone. "Do you have any tickets on your record, any accidents you want to tell me about?"

"No."

"All right, then." He finished the transaction and slid the phone into his pocket before going to the lockbox on the wall. Opening it, he took out a set of keys and tossed them to her. She stared at them as if she'd never seen such things. "For the time being, you'll drive the coupe. When Brooks says you're well enough and strong enough to go on your way, we'll figure out some other transportation for you. Something safer and drier than a moped. Agreed?"

She gulped and blinked. "I, um, I've already put on some weight."

"Yeah?" He had noticed. He wished he hadn't, but he had.

She rubbed her nose and blinked some more. "You know, I sometimes think you are the most insufferably high-handed, arrogant, bossiest... Then you go and do something so kind and generous." She looked up, her gray eyes large and luminous and brimming. "Thank you." Before he knew what was happening, she'd thrown her arms around his neck.

She went up on tiptoe and pulled his head down to kiss his cheek, right at the corner of his mouth. Then he did something incredibly stupid. He turned his head just a tad, and she pressed her lips to his.

He felt poleaxed, stunned. It was a wonder they didn't both just topple over backward. As it was, he stumbled slightly.

No longer the cool, urbane college professor, he hadn't felt so stupid since...ever. As if he'd just had his first kiss at the ripe old age of forty-five. Horrified, he leaped away.

"You can...give it back...later," he managed, trying for an authoritative tone.

She showed him her apple cheeks. "I'll be very careful, I promise."

"Yes." He fought the urge to clear his throat. "See that you are."

He loped down the length of the building and punched the garage door opener on the other end. She got into the car, tossing her backpack in ahead of her, started the engine and pulled up level with him. The window rolled down, and she regarded him solemnly.

"I don't know how to thank you."

"It's late," he grumbled. "Get on."

She gave him a slow smile, as if she knew that his heart still pounded like a jackhammer, before carefully easing the car out into the night. He hit the button and watched the door slide down behind her, then he bent at the waist, grabbed his knees and gasped for air.

What was wrong with him? He had to get a hold of himself. Simone had been through so much, and he felt sorry for her, but that was all it was, all it could be. She was a student and too young for him. Much too young. It was absurd for him to get so worked up over a little kiss of gratitude like this.

Which didn't make him feel any less like a heel.

Chapter Seven

Simone still couldn't quite believe that Morgan had just handed over the keys to a sweet little coupe to her. And to think that he'd put her on his insurance! It couldn't have cost much—could it?—and it was better to be safe than sorry, but she hadn't been able to sleep that night for thinking about what an incredibly generous thing he'd done. At least that was what she tried to tell herself.

What she kept picturing, what she kept reliving, as she lay there in that comfortable bed in that lovely, quiet room in Chatam House, was the kiss.

She'd only meant to hug him, and then on impulse she'd kissed his cheek, and somehow their lips had met. The feeling had somehow caught her off guard. He was so solid. So…manly. Aaron, her ex, seemed like a rather pathetic child by comparison, and that saddened her, made him, her and their marriage seem like such a farce.

All during class on Friday morning, she found it difficult to concentrate. Her gaze kept straying where it should not go, and she found herself fascinated with the cleft in Morgan, rather, *Professor* Chatam's chin. It was embarrassing, really, and she couldn't help wondering how many other female students were as captivated by that little indentation as she was. She practically ran from the lecture hall at the end of class, aware of his silent gaze tracking her.

She felt more than a bit odd driving over to the mission in Morgan's car, but though Hub surely recognized the vehicle, he said nothing. His comments all concerned the news that an Arlington theme park had donated a dozen tickets and meals for a special promotion a week from the following Saturday. The church would provide a fifteen-passenger van, but at least two people, a driver and a monitor, would have to go along with the teens.

"Oh, Hub. These kids never get to do things like this," Simone said excitedly. "What fun they would have!"

"I know, but I almost didn't mention it," he told her. "I'm too old for this sort of thing, you know, and I'm not sure you have the stamina for it."

She wasn't sure, either. A venture like this would require a whole day, twelve hours from open to close of the park. Still, she could imagine the joy on the faces of those teenagers. She could also imagine what Morgan would say if he found out. Unless…

"You don't suppose that Morgan would agree to help out, do you?"

Hub folded his hands and smiled. "Well, now, you never know until you ask. And I might have a way to twist his arm a bit."

"Roller coasters," Morgan repeated, standing on the terra-cotta floor of his small foyer in his bare feet the next morning, his hair still damp from a shower and his cheeks still smarting from the aftershave he'd splashed on. His Saturday jeans felt as comfortable and familiar as his collared knit shirt, the tail of which he hadn't yet stuffed into his waistband. He'd been quite surprised to find Simone knocking at his door, but the proposition that she had poured out had him reeling.

"The longest, highest and fastest in the world," she confirmed eagerly.

"And you want to ride them?"

"No, not me," she said, shaking her head. "You. And the kids. You know, teenagers. Young people. From the mission."

It started coalescing. He'd heard something in there about donated tickets and special promotions and *fun*.

"Aha. You want to palm off your homeless kids on me."

"No! Not at all. I'll go along. It's just that I can't do this for them by myself." She gave him the most woebegone, puppy-dog face. "And your dad isn't up to it, not at his age, and, well, everyone else I know is busy with work or other assignments, and I certainly can't ask your aunts." He chuckled at the thought of Odelia, Hypatia and Magnolia shepherding a flock of world-wise teenagers around an amusement park, and that seemed to embolden Simone. "The kids would so love it. You can't know what this would mean to them."

He knew without a doubt that he should turn her down flat. The last thing he ought to do was spend an entire day in her company, but he didn't really see that he had any other choice. If he didn't do this, she'd just find someone else or try it all on her own. He supposed he could tap a couple of students to help out, but he couldn't trust them not to let her overdo. He wondered if Brooks might be available and instantly nixed that idea, uncomfortable with it for reasons he didn't want to ponder. Besides, he did love a good roller coaster.

"You're not to overdo," he dictated, folding his arms.

A wide grin split her face. "I won't. I promise. I'll pace myself. I'll sit at every opportunity. I have several books on my phone so I can read. It won't be a problem."

He shook his head, which needed a thorough examination, and asked, "How many young people are we expecting?"

"I don't know. As many as ten, maybe."

"I'd better see if I can round up a couple extra sets of eyes and ears, then."

"Could you?"

"I do know a few graduate students."

"Oh, Morgan, you're wonderful. You're just wonderful. Forget all those things I said about you being bossy and high-handed and autocratic."

He frowned. He didn't mean it, but he frowned. "I don't think I heard autocratic. I did hear arrogant and insufferable."

"Well, those still apply," she teased, all but dancing across the foyer. "You can forget the rest, though."

He chuckled. "We'll see what you say after I drag you onto the roller coaster."

Her eyes grew round. "Oh, no." She wagged a finger at him as she backed through the door, pulling it closed behind her. "No, no, no."

He just grinned. *Yes, yes, yes.*

"No, no, no." Simone shook her head.

She was glad that they'd heeded the gate attendant's advice to head clear across the park to the Big Daddy roller coaster at the back. He'd promised them that the wait would be shortest if they started at the back of the hundred-acre park and worked their way forward rather than the other way around. He'd warned that wait times per ride could exceed two hours otherwise. Because they'd been waiting in line when the gates opened, they were first in line now, and their party of fourteen—she suspected Morgan had shelled out the nearly two hundred bucks for the two extra tickets—comprised of nine males and five females, was raring to go, all but her and Rina, who had disappeared into a bathroom.

"Winded already?" Morgan asked, watching the others run ahead to get in line.

It had been a long walk, but she wasn't going to admit to weakness already. "No, I just don't care for fast rides."

He cocked his head. "Really? I thought you were a skier."

"Yes, but on the slopes, I'm in control."

"Control freak, huh?"

Ouch. If she'd learned one thing during her illness, however, it was how little control she actually had in life. "No. That would be you."

He lifted a shoulder, gave his head a shake. "Don't see me sitting on the sidelines."

She squelched a sigh, admitting, "I distrust large mechanical contraptions."

"Huh. Never rode a ski lift, then. Odd."

"Of course I've ridden ski lifts."

"I guarantee you they're far less safe than this thing is."

"You can't know that."

"I can, actually. I've read the studies."

"You are exasperating."

"You are illogical," he retorted. "You zip around town on a fragile little two-wheeler that any nearsighted granny or distracted teenager can easily cremate, then worry about getting on one of the engineering wonders of the modern world. Come on. I'll hold your hand."

"Bully," she grumbled, casually letting her hand fall at her side as she trudged to the entry.

"Coward," he replied cheerfully, catching her palm against his as he matched his stride to hers. "You'll like it."

"Ha."

She didn't look at him, pretending displeasure as he tugged her up the ramp to the covered platform, where they negotiated a maze of roped-off lines to finally file into narrow spaces between numbered pipes at the edge of the rails. Vaguely aware of the hissing and clashing of hydraulics and metal parts, she didn't really see or feel anything that wasn't centered on the hand that he clutched in his, until suddenly a long line of sleek, linked cars painted a fiery red shot past them and came to a screeching, jarring halt.

With a whoosh of steam and the clank of metal, a padded bar popped up, revealing two molded seats below. They looked like something out of a space capsule, without nearly enough capsule to protect them. Simone instinctively pulled back.

"Oh, I don't think so."

"Honey, you're holding up the line," Morgan said close to her ear. Then he simply picked her up and stepped down into the car with her. She didn't even have time to grab hold of his neck before he deposited her in the outer seat and dropped down next to her. Sputtering, she gaped at him, but he just pulled down his three-point harness and snapped it closed, saying, "Buckle up, sweetheart. We're about to ride."

Before she could tell him what he could do with his ride, buckles and all, an attendant swept by and checked her harness. Then the padded bar came down over her head, and the same attendant used his foot to lock it tightly into place against her thighs. The car lurched and slowly rolled forward, gradually picking up speed as it came toward a first precipitate drop.

Simone cut her eyes at Morgan and promised, "I am going to get you for this."

He clasped her hand in his, grinned and said, "Okay," just as the bottom dropped out from under them.

She screamed like a lunatic and couldn't seem to stop. He laughed, loud and long and heartily, and not once did he let go of her hand.

After what seemed an eternity, or perhaps three minutes, of rolls and flips and mind-boggling drops and curves, they arrived right back where they'd started. The car came to a screeching, jarring halt, and she had just enough time to catch her breath before the padded bar whooshed up. Morgan released his belt and let go of her hand in order to release hers. They had to exit on her side, so she started to push herself up, but then she felt Morgan's hands under her arms, lifting her. The others of their party, in cars ahead of them, had already exited, laughing, down the covered ramp to their right.

"My legs are like jelly," she complained, stepping up onto the platform.

Laughing happily, he hopped up beside her. "I'll carry you, then." He swept her off her feet and spun with her before heading down the ramp.

She set her arms about his neck, smiling. He seemed so open and happy, his cinnamon eyes completely unguarded today. "You make it awfully difficult to stay angry with you, but you can't always carry me."

"Yes, I can," he refuted gaily, but reality waited at the bottom of the ramp, and it smacked her hard in the chest. It wouldn't do for the other graduate students to see them like this. She'd already read the policy in her student handbook and heard it giggled about by the girls on campus.

"What a shame the professors can't date students."

"If ever you were going to break the rules, that not-fooling-around-with-the-professors thing would be it, wouldn't it?"

"A professor would have to really be in love with you to risk his job for you."

"No," she said softly, dropping her gaze, "you can't."

He stopped and, a heartbeat later, let her down.

"You're right," he said, the professor again. "Good call."

Nodding, she adjusted the hem of the little mint-green T-shirt that she wore over lightweight olive cargo pants and her most comfortable athletic shoes. Then she turned and calmly walked down the ramp and out into sunshine that seemed to have lost some of its luster.

As the day wore on, everyone appeared to have a great time—everyone but Rina. Simone wondered why the girl had even come. She refused to ride any of the rides and sat morosely during all the shows. Only as they were leaving a particularly crowded musical, while killing time before their dinner reservations, did Simone realize the problem. It happened because two of the guys were clowning around, hopping back and forth on the carpeted, backless concrete benches where they'd sat to watch the stage show. One of them bumped into Rina from the back, knocking her forward into Simone. It was with shock that Simone felt Rina collide against her. Rina's was not the soft, mushy body of the overweight but the hard, distended belly of the pregnant.

In a flash, Simone realized the problem. Rina wasn't tubby; she was expecting a baby, and the oversize clothes were meant to disguise that fact, which they had done fairly successfully thus far, aided by Rina's round face and sullen expression. Simone suddenly recognized how small and delicate the girl's hands and feet were compared to her girth. She saw, too, the flash of fear in Rina's blue eyes. Slumping, the girl muttered something unkind to the boys and slung an elbow at one of them.

Simone did her best to remain impassive, saying calmly, "No harm done. But you probably ought to cool it, guys, before they kick us out of here."

Morgan, who was two or three bodies ahead of them in the line trying to push out into the crush of the aisle, looked back over his shoulder and asked, "Everyone okay?"

"Sure," Simone said. "Hungry." And tired. She was abruptly weary. All of a sudden, it seemed that every other female she met was going to have a baby. She tried not to think about it.

They eventually made their way out of the theater and across the way to the restaurant where they had vouchers. By the time they were finally showed to their seats, she was absolutely exhausted with waiting and not thinking. Night had fallen, and with it came a cool, light breeze. Simone pulled a rumpled beige powder jacket from a communal backpack toted by the guys in the group. It sported a hot-pink oversize zipper and cuffs and collar. With the collar turned up, it kept her quite cozy, so she didn't mind that the table to which their party was showed stood in the open air. They were served a decent meal of grilled chicken, rice, green beans, salad and apple cobbler, a definite improvement over the dry, cold hamburger and fries she hadn't had much interest in at lunch, but she was too tired to really do the dinner justice. She caught herself nodding off over a cup of cocoa, and when she looked up, Morgan was sitting on the bench next to her.

"I think you're done."

"I am tired," she admitted. She had promised, after all, not to overdo. "I'll just find a place to sit while the rest of you finish up."

To her surprise, the kids themselves objected, saying they were ready to leave the park at any time. She knew that there were rides and exhibits yet in which several of them had expressed interest, so she shook her head.

"I'm perfectly content to sit and wait."

"Tell you what," Morgan said, "I think we could wrap this up in about an hour if we use a little organization." He quickly ascertained who wanted to do what and split the party into groups, sending them off with instructions to meet back at the main gate in an hour's time or as close to it as possible. He then asked Rina to stay with Simone and set out on his own, returning about twenty minutes later with a wheelchair.

Simone grimaced. "I'm not crippled," she protested.

"I'm well aware of that fact," he told her. "Humor me."

She glanced at Rina, wishing she could countermand the chair for the girl, but unable to do so without revealing her pregnancy.

"Hey," Rina said, "if some dude got a wheelchair for me, I'd ride in it."

"Well, then, you take it," Simone proposed hopefully.

"Uh-uh." Rina refused, grinning at Morgan. "I said some dude, not some uptight college professor."

"Rina!" Simone scolded, trying not to laugh.

"The uptight college professor wants the exhausted graduate student in the chair," Morgan ordered. "The rude teenager can walk."

"Y'all take your time," Rina said, trudging off with a wave. "I gotta make a pit stop. I'll catch you at the front gate."

Simone sighed and got in the chair.

"That is one strange young woman," Morgan muttered as he pushed the chair forward.

"It's not what you think," Simone told him.

"You don't know what I think," he retorted softly.

She knew that even in a grossly unfair world it was possible to have exhaustingly wonderful days that left her equally torn between tears and laughter.

* * *

Someone should kick him. No one would, so Morgan mentally kicked himself. How could he allow her to exhaust herself like this? He couldn't seem to get it right with her. He either got too close or he kept too much distance to realize when she needed protection. Her fragility was evident, but he'd let her go gallivanting all over town on a moped, of all things, and in the rain, and now she'd worn herself out at an amusement park, just as he had predicted and *while he was with her,* but he'd been so busy trying not to notice everything about her that he'd missed the most important thing. He wanted to howl with frustration.

She was always subdued, almost regally so, but her quietness tonight almost frightened him. Something had happened. Something had changed.

Who was he kidding? Everything had changed.

He didn't know for sure when it had happened. Maybe when he'd picked her up and put her on that roller coaster, maybe when he'd taken her hand. Maybe when she'd kissed him that night in his garage. Maybe even before that. All he knew was that he couldn't seem to get his equilibrium with her. He was either too close or too far. Or maybe he hadn't gotten close enough yet, and that was what really frightened him.

Never before had he pushed anyone onto a roller coaster or anything remotely resembling one. But he'd wanted so badly to share that with her, something he loved, something he craved, something he really got a big kick out of, and for all her protestations, she'd had a blast with it. Still, he shouldn't have done it, just as he shouldn't have let her wear herself out.

She leaned her head against the window of the van and was asleep before they got out of the parking lot, which was vast. The kids were great about it. They'd had quite a day and were ebullient, but they talked softly among themselves or not at all as he drove them back to Buffalo Creek. Rina sat alone, staring at Simone and occasionally at him, as if trying to puzzle something out.

Join the club, he thought.

He dropped off everyone at the mission, everyone but Simone, who slept so soundly that she didn't wake until he gathered her into his arms to carry her up the walkway in front of Chatam House, where he'd picked her up that morning.

"Oh, are we there?"

"Um-hmm."

"Good."

Her arm about his neck, she laid her head on his shoulder and emitted a soft, snuffling snore. He grinned.

"You can't always carry me," she'd said.

"Yes, I can," he whispered.

He couldn't, of course. He shouldn't. He wouldn't. Oh, but he wanted to.

He carried her into the house, pushing the door closed with his foot, across the grand foyer and up the great staircase.

This just got more and more dangerous all the time.

She was a student. He loved his job; it was his calling. There were rules about professors and students.

She was too young for him. Much too young. Almost twenty years too young. Well, fifteen. Okay, ten. Ten years too young.

She'd been dreadfully ill, with cancer. He'd already lost too much to cancer.

Morgan carried Simone along the landing to her room at the back of the house, dipped slightly to open the door, then stopped. His aunts were no doubt sleeping. The staff would have retired to the carriage house hours ago. There was no one to see him go into Simone's room, but he wouldn't do that. Instead of setting her on her feet, however, he shrugged his shoulder.

"Wake up, sleepyhead. You're home."

"Home," she said groggily.

"Home," he repeated, so very thankful to have her safe at Chatam House.

She sucked in a deep breath, kicked a foot, glanced around her. The bright deep pink collar of her jacket framed her lovely face. Her gaze came back to his, and she said softly, "You're carrying me again."

"So I am," he told her, aware that his face was too close to hers, their noses all but touching.

She made a helpless sound, tilted her head slightly and kissed him, her hands sliding up the nape of his neck. He'd never felt quite so happy, so he kissed her back, deeply, joyously, unwisely. He felt like the most powerful man on earth, standing there with his feet braced wide apart, holding her in his arms, cradled against his chest, kissing her, feeling her delicate hands slip possessively about his head. She cupped his ears, sifted her fingers through his hair, measured the shape and size of his skull, as if storing up memories to savor, while he marveled that he should feel such things for this girl, this student, who could cost him everything. She was too young, too broken, too dangerous. And somehow perfect.

He didn't know who pulled back first. Perhaps it was mutual. One moment their lips were melded, and then their foreheads were touching. Finally, he had to let her down.

Tears stood in her glorious eyes, but she wouldn't shed them. He knew instinctively that no tears would fall. She was strong enough to hold them back. A part of him was glad; another part resented it greatly. She had been through much, but he was nineteen years her senior, by far the wiser of them, and torn to shreds inside. He had loved and lost in the cruelest of ways, and just as his father had buried two wives, he had buried two mothers. Yet here she stood, as fragile as eggshell outside but as strong as tempered steel inside. She was enough to make him want to risk it all, when he knew, *knew* how disastrous that would be.

He skimmed a hand over her cheek and said, "That cannot happen again."

Then he left her as quietly and quickly as possible, shaken to his core.

Chapter Eight

Morgan and his father had always had a good relationship. For that matter, Morgan was on good terms with everyone in the family. Bayard, the oldest of Hubner's four children, was a dutiful if somewhat distant son and brother, his and Morgan's mother, Ardis, having died in a silly accident when Morgan was ten.

Their younger siblings, Chandler and Kaylie, were the children of their stepmother, or "second mom," Kathryn. She had been pure joy, and Hub had cratered after her death from cancer. He'd aged twenty years in two and had chained Kaylie, a nurse, to him with guilt, fighting with Chandler over every little thing.

Thankfully, those days were behind them. Chandler and his wife, Bethany, were happily raising their son on a prosperous horse ranch in Stephenville. When Kaylie had married, she'd planned for

Hub to live with her and Stephen. Hub had insisted, however, that he would have his own space, so they'd built him an apartment with a private entrance.

Hub, eldest Chatam, former pastor, father, grand-father, twice-widowed husband, was himself again, a wise and caring man, so even at forty-five years of age Morgan didn't hesitate to go to his dad when he had a problem that he couldn't solve alone. He waited until after the morning service on Sunday, shamefully glad that Simone had not come even if the aunties had scolded him for letting her tire her-self out the day before, before he tooled up the im-pressive drive of Kaylie and Stephen's soaring house on the southwest outskirts of Buffalo Creek, seeking wisdom and strength and confirmation, he supposed, of what he knew was right and best.

He drove around to the far end of the house and parked in front of the single-bay garage where his dad kept his old car. Hub steadfastly refused to allow Stephen to buy him another, saying that he could buy his own anytime he wished, which was true. Morgan got out of the BMW—it had seemed the appropri-ate auto for this address—and walked up to knock on his father's door.

Hub answered a few moments later in his house slippers and suspenders, blinking owlishly behind the lenses of his wire-framed glasses. "Morgan! What brings you out this way, son?"

"Simone," he answered simply.

"Ah." Hub nodded in understanding, almost as if he'd been expecting this visit and its subject matter. "Come in. Let's talk it through."

He led the way down a terrazzo-tiled hallway, bypassing a tiny, barely used kitchen on the way to a comfortable sitting room with a cheery gas blaze in a lovely rock fireplace. A wall of glass overlooked a professionally maintained garden in the backyard, and a large flat-screen TV took up another.

"You find her a temptation," Hub surmised, waving Morgan into a seat on the comfortable leather sofa.

"To put it mildly."

Hub chuckled, sounding genuinely pleased. Morgan came right back up off the sofa to pace the room with agitated strides.

"It's not a laughing matter! I could lose my job over this. You know what strict policies are in place for Bible College professors."

"Yes, of course, and rightly so," Hub said solemnly. "But the strictest policies concern undergraduate students."

Stopping in midstride, Morgan gaped at him. "What's that supposed to mean?"

"Obviously, Simone is a graduate student, and mature for her age, I'd say. I like her."

Morgan glared at him, astonished. "You're not helping! I expected a stern lecture…"

"Great lot of good those do," Hub muttered.

"…a helpful meditation exercise…"

"Oh, those I have in abundance. But so do you."

"…maybe even a stunning insight into midlife crisis."

Hub shook his head, brow furrowed. "You know, I've never figured out when midlife is. I don't think anyone does until it's long past."

Morgan dropped down onto the sofa again, his head in his hands. "I'm terrified that I'm going to do something stupid, and you're talking esoteric nonsense!"

"Morgan," Hub said calmly, "half your problem is that you haven't done anything truly stupid in decades."

Morgan looked up sharply at that. "Well, how's this for stupid? I keep kissing her!" Hub beamed so brightly that Morgan felt duty bound to amend the statement. "Actually, she keeps kissing me, and I sort of kiss her back."

"And why is that?" Hub asked with a face as straight as a plumb line.

"Because I want to," Morgan admitted baldly. "Because I like how it makes me feel."

"And how is that?" Hub asked.

Morgan threw out his arms in disgust. "Like I'm ten feet tall and able to leap tall buildings in a single bound!"

Hub clucked his tongue. "Oh, that's terrible."

"No, that's wonderful. But it's all wrong, Dad, for

so many reasons. It's not just my job or my career that we're talking about. It's my *calling*. If I'm not true to that, I'm not true to God."

And there it was, the worst of it, the thing that frightened him most. Morgan rubbed his hands over his face. Could he really be tempted to so grievous a failing? His father seemed to think so.

"This I understand," Hub told him soberly.

"And she's so very young," Morgan went on, eager to lay it all out now. "I know Kathryn was younger than you—"

"Nineteen years."

"Really? That much *exactly?*" Morgan was surprised. He'd thought fifteen years or so. At every birthday, they'd joked about keeping her age a secret, and everyone had known it was because of the age difference between them, but somehow it hadn't seemed important, especially as she had died first. It had been five, six years now since her passing. Whoa. Time passed so quickly.

"Gave me pause," Hub was saying, "but I had you, and you needed a mother."

"She was a wonderful mother," Morgan said, smiling.

"And a wonderful wife, and I'll tell you what she told me when I balked. You come to a point where you're either both adults or you're not, and she figured she'd given me long enough to mature."

Morgan could just hear Kathryn saying it. He

hadn't been quite eleven years old when they'd married, but it had seemed to him that she had made his careworn father younger with her vibrant love and personality. The whole church had been abuzz with talk that Kathryn had pursued the widowed minister, and she'd freely admitted it.

Simone was not Kathryn, however. They were as different as night and day. Kathryn had been all flutter and gaiety, all sparkle and whirlwind; Simone was quiet, self-possessed, sometimes stormy, sometimes a serene zephyr, a little mysterious, often unexpected. Kathryn had always left Morgan feeling stuffed with her presence; Simone left him wanting more, as if he couldn't get quite enough of her. It disturbed him, that feeling, worried him. He feared that she could become an addiction.

"There are things you don't know, Dad," Morgan said softly, aware that he was betraying a confidence. "Please don't tell anyone else."

"I'm adding pastor's vestments to my father's mantle now," Hub told him in all seriousness.

"Simone cannot have children. She's had cancer."

Hub winced at the news. "Dread disease."

"That's why I've been so concerned about her. Brooks says she's beaten it and just needs time to recover."

"But the specter is always there, especially after Brigitte and your stepmother."

"It's not that so much," Morgan said, realizing that

was true, "but realistically speaking, for Simone to have children, she will need to adopt."

"And you're too old to begin that process in the normal way of things," Hub surmised. "Yes, I see. But, Morgan, we've gone from kissing to marriage and raising children in a single conversation."

"I seem to recall you telling me that's where kissing leads," Morgan teased, feeling better for simply having it all said aloud now.

Hub chuckled. "So I did, and so it does. But there is a little thing called courtship first."

"Yowza," Morgan joked, "maybe in a past generation."

"You know what I mean."

"And that brings us full circle to right back where we started. BCBC has clear-cut policies against professors and students dating or otherwise becoming romantically involved."

Hub tapped a finger against the cleft in his chin. "I seem to recall a few exceptions to that rule."

"Spouses who enroll as students. Faculty who are also students. That's about it."

Hubner spread his hands. "Is there no faculty position for which Simone might be qualified? The good Lord knows we don't pay her enough to keep body and soul together at the mission. She'd starve if she wasn't with your aunts."

Morgan shook his head. "That wouldn't be a true solution. It would only take care of one problem."

"Well, we'll pray about it," Hub said. "There's your only real solution, anyway."

"I know, Dad," Morgan told him. "I feel better with you praying about it, too."

"That's what I'm here for," Hub told him warmly, "to pray for my children. It's my burden and my privilege, as much my calling as the pastorate ever has been, a joy among sorrows, more precious to me than jewels."

For the first time, Morgan felt a definite pang at his lack of offspring. He prayed for his students, of course. Simone was just one for whom he'd prayed over the years. Many more would need his care and concern in the years ahead. Which was all the reason he needed to avoid temptation and protect his calling. Why did it suddenly feel like such a gargantuan task?

She lay in wait like a thief, and in her own house, no less, but Hypatia felt compelled to have a private word with Simone. The child had looked like death warmed over on Sunday morning, with dark circles under her eyes and an alarming pallor. Clearly the trip to the amusement park—Hub had told them all about it—had been too much for Simone. Hypatia had seen no choice but to press the girl to stay home in bed, and she'd felt quite put out with her nephew about it. She'd thought that Morgan, above all others, could be trusted to see to it that Simone did not overtax herself, but there the poor thing had stood, looking on the verge of collapse.

"I'll have a word with Morgan Charles Chatam," Hypatia had announced, feeling Simone's forehead for sign of a fever. "What was he thinking to let you get into such a state?"

"Were there roller coasters involved?" Odelia had asked, all worried curiosity. Roller coasters! Hubner seemed to find Morgan's fascination with the things amusing, but Hypatia couldn't help thinking that it was rather undignified for a grown man.

Simone's reaction had been most telling, however. She had paled even whiter, before her face had bloomed bloodred, and she had grabbed Hypatia's hand in both of hers, imploring her, "Oh, no, you mustn't blame Morg—er, Professor Chatam. He was such help to me! He's always been so very much help to me."

Hypatia had exchanged a glance with her tittering, romantically minded sister, then quickly shooed the same from the room. It wouldn't do to have Odelia building love affairs out of blushes and chance remarks, but Hypatia hadn't been able to dismiss so lightly the troubled softness in Simone's tired gray eyes or her concerns about a developing relationship. A crush on Simone's part was one thing; anything more could be catastrophic.

She lifted the edge of the lavender silk sleeve at her wrist and checked the time on the face of her watch.

If Simone proved true to form, she'd be coming down those stairs anytime now on her way to Monday morning class. Morgan's class. Simone never missed it. On occasion, she skipped one or the other of her classes but never, apparently, Morgan's. That could be because Morgan's class was a prerequisite for her acceptance into the graduate program, or it could be because Simone felt a debt of gratitude toward him. Or it could be…

Hypatia frowned. She was not given to romantic nonsense herself, but even she had to admit, secretly, that of all her nephews Morgan was by far the most appealing. Everyone knew that half the females on campus threw themselves at his feet every semester without fail, but stalwart fellow that he was, he had remained true to his calling and the memory of his Brigitte. Hypatia had always considered him a Chatam after her own heart, happy in his single state. Now she feared that Simone might upset that balance a bit, and someone could get hurt, perhaps Simone, perhaps Morgan, perhaps both.

Simone came skipping down the stairs in a whispered rush, her tread so light that Hypatia would have missed her if she'd waited in the parlor or library as she'd considered doing. Calmly rounding the curved post at the foot of the staircase, Hypatia put on a welcoming smile.

"There you are. Looking fit, I see, and feeling better, I trust."

Simone drew up on the bottom step, smiling down at Hypatia. She looked slim and sleek but healthy in wheat-colored jeans and a matching hooded jacket worn over a bright orange T-shirt and orange canvas shoes, the ubiquitous backpack slung over one shoulder. "Thank you. I feel well."

"That bag looks heavy."

"It is, but I only carry it to and from the car." She leaned forward, winking conspiratorially, and added, "Don't tell the professor. He gave me a rolling case some time ago, and it's a great help on campus, but it's more trouble to lug up and down the stairs than the backpack."

"He does try to see to your needs," Hypatia mused.

"Oh, yes. He's very kind."

"And you are falling in love with him," Hypatia ventured gently.

Simone seemed more dismayed than shocked. "Ma'am," she said carefully, "you know that students cannot date professors. It's strictly forbidden."

"And that has precisely what to do with your feelings?" Hypatia asked in a kind tone.

Licking her lips, Simone let down the backpack. She seemed to be breathing with some difficulty. "I—I'm trying to explain to you that I can't have feelings for Professor Chatam."

"Of course you can," Hypatia refuted. "Perhaps you should not—"

"Must not," Simone interrupted firmly. "I *must*

not have feelings for him. You see, it isn't just that I am forbidden to involve myself with him, it's that I could never give him—" she looked down "—any of the things that other women can."

Bemused, Hypatia asked, "Such as?"

"Children," Simone answered in a husky whisper. "I can never give him a child, which he surely deserves."

Surprised but not unduly troubled by this admission, Hypatia nodded. So the cancer had taken that choice from her. How sad for her. Still, not every woman chose to be a parent, herself included, and not every man.

"I've never known Morgan to voice a yearning or even a preference for children."

Simone looked up in surprise. "Oh, but he's so wonderful with them. You should have seen him with the kids in my group on Saturday! Granted, they aren't little children. Some of them are actually adults. Or should be. But I see him around campus, and Saturday with the children in the park, little strangers running wild, he was so patient, so indulgent. I think he had more fun than they did. I saw all these exasperated fathers, dragging their little kiddies around by the arms and threatening them with shaking fingers, and I thought, 'Morgan wouldn't be like that. Morgan would know what to say and do to make them *want* to obey.' *I* may want to smack him sometimes, but he'd be a wonderful dad. I know it." She smiled to herself, and Hypatia felt her heart turn over.

Couldn't or *shouldn't* didn't matter. Simone had answered Hypatia's questions without even meaning to, and her heart bled for the girl.

"One wonders how he feels about you," she heard herself say, wishing that she could call back the words, but Simone merely shook her head.

"It doesn't matter," she said, stepping down onto the foyer floor. "Whatever he might feel for me now, he wouldn't if he knew all there is to know."

Hypatia tilted her head, studying that piquant face. Something about the eyes—or was it the cheekbones?—struck her as oddly familiar, but she couldn't quite... Perhaps it was the sadness, such a depth of sadness. They'd certainly had a season of sadness in this house not too long ago, but joy had followed it. Hypatia trusted that such would be the case again, for the psalmist said that those who sowed with tears would reap with songs of joy, and so it had proven time and again.

"I think perhaps you underestimate both Morgan and our Lord," Hypatia said at length, speaking as much to herself as to Simone. She tried on a smile and said, "Why don't we just pray about it and see what God has in store, hmm?"

Simone smiled, nodding, but Hypatia could see that her heart wasn't really in it. She wasn't convinced that anything could change. It must seem to her that God had spoken already, that His will had been done when the cancer had taken certain female organs. Hypatia wondered again how likely it was that Simone's cancer would return.

Mumbling that she had to get to class, Simone dragged the backpack from the step and shouldered it before sweeping around the end of the staircase and hurrying off toward the back of the house.

Perhaps Simone was not the one for whom she should have lain in wait. She turned smartly on her heeled pump and marched into the parlor, where Magnolia and Odelia were enjoying their morning tea.

"Oh, sisters," she announced, "we have some serious praying to do."

After her unexpected conversation with Hypatia, staying away from Chatam House and the Chatams—Morgan, especially—seemed Simone's best course of action. She had plenty to do. Her studies and her work at the mission were enough to keep her away. After check-in at the mission the following night, Simone saw her ministry partner off, locked the doors and settled into the office that Hub had set up for her.

Humming to herself, she mentally blocked out the cavernous building beyond the flimsy walls of her utilitarian workspace and concentrated on the paper that she was writing for one of her classes. So deep in thought was she that the first knock—though no more, really, than a pat on the door—sounded like a cannon shot to her. She jerked and knocked over a cup of paper clips, scattering them across the desktop. A flurry of knocks followed, accompanied by a pair of sobs.

Simone shot to her feet and made it out into the corridor before she remembered to go back for her cell phone. Clutching the tiny safeguard, she keyed in the numbers 9-1-1, then, with her thumb poised over the call button, she quickly advanced on the brown metal door, calling out, "Who's there?"

"It's Rina!" came a muffled but unmistakably feminine voice. "Simone, is that you? Let me in. Oh, please let me in."

Hearing the soft cries on the other side of the door, Simone quickly stowed the phone in a pocket and opened up. Rina stumbled inside, her arms wrapped protectively about her middle.

"Are you in labor?"

Her pale head jerked up at the question, but after only a moment's hesitation, she shook it firmly. "No. No pains. I got away before he really hurt me. But he punched me. He punched me in the stomach!"

He, whoever he was, had punched her in the face, too. She had a split lip and a lump below her left eye, as well as a bruise on her chin.

Simone slid an arm around the girl and helped her into the small kitchen. "Who did this to you?"

"It doesn't matter. I was stupid to go back."

"Was it the baby's father?" Simone asked, pushing the girl down onto a stool next to the deep metal sink.

"He wants me to kill it! I keep thinking he'll change his mind, but he just says to get rid of it or he will."

Simone closed her eyes and counted to ten slowly. "When you refused, he tried to beat you into a miscarriage. Am I right?"

Rina sighed and nodded. "He's got other kids, and the state garnishes his paycheck for child support, so he don't want no more. I worked for a while, but I got laid off, and I'm too far along to get hired now. That's why I went back. I thought maybe, at this stage, he'd give me some time until the baby comes and I could work again, but he's still insisting on an abortion."

Simone took a deep breath. "I'm glad you chose life for your baby, Rina. I know I'm probably prejudiced because I can't have children, but I think it's very brave of you, and I'll help any way I can."

"Oh, no," Rina said, suddenly all compassion. "You can't have kids?"

Simone shook her head, not trusting herself to speak.

"And you're so nice."

Simone had to smile. "Thank you. But nice doesn't make you a mother."

"What happened?"

"It was cancer."

"Man, that stinks!"

"Yes, it does," Simone agreed, suddenly desperate to change the subject. "Uh, when is the baby due?"

Rina shrugged. "I'm really not sure. January, I think."

"You haven't been to a doctor?"

Rina shook her head. "I didn't have no money, and I guess I was just too embarrassed, not being married, and my boyfriend wanting to kill it and all."

"Well, that's past," Simone said. "Right now, we have to make sure you're safe. Then we'll get you the prenatal care you need. Where have you been staying?"

"Oh, here and there, one shelter or another, but I can't stay there no more. He'll find me now he knows I didn't go back to my folks in Kansas like I said I was going to."

"Why didn't you?" Simone asked, thinking that might be a solution.

"I was going to," Rina told her miserably, "but my mama's sick, and my daddy's got her and my grandma there to take care of already. Her mind's bad, and she don't know who I am anymore. I scare her. It don't seem right to upset everybody because I'm so stupid as to get myself into this mess. Besides, the house is so small, I'd be sleeping on the couch, anyway."

Simone sighed. "It's all right. I'll take care of you." *Somehow.* Thinking quickly, she added, "You'll have to stay in the emergency room. Just be sure you're out of there by the time Pastor Chatam opens up tomorrow around lunch."

"Oh, thank you! I'll do just as you say," Rina promised, "but do you think I could get something to eat? I'm hungry all the time now."

"Of course," Simone said, turning toward the pantry. "We only keep snacks here, though. Tomorrow I'll make sure you get some really nutritious food. And I'm making a doctor's appointment for you."

"All right."

"We'll do this together," Simone promised, smiling at the hope that filled Rina's eyes.

Simone knew that she was breaking all the rules. She should be turning this over to the authorities, not hiding Rina, but the wheels of government often ground slowly. What if Rina's abuser should catch up with her before she could be gotten into a safe situation? The authorities could handle the matter once this baby was safely born. Until then, Simone would do what she had to. If she couldn't be a mother, at least she could make sure that someone else could be.

And maybe, just maybe, that was the point of it all.

Chapter Nine

"Are you all right?"

Simone jumped and whirled, stumbling against the curb, the hand holding the car keys going to the center of her chest. "Morg— *Professor*. You startled me."

"I can see that, but I don't understand it. I've been following you and calling your name halfway across campus."

Her gaze slid away from his. "I, uh, didn't hear you."

"No kidding. You also didn't answer my question."

She offered him a weak smile. "Sorry. Say again."

He raked his gaze over her. She had lost weight, only a bit, but enough to alarm him. "Are you ill?"

"No. I'm fine."

"You've lost a few pounds."

She rolled her eyes. "I'm one of those disgusting people who can miss a meal and inadvertently drop pounds."

"And why have you been missing meals?" he asked, frowning.

She put out a stilted laugh. "I've been busy, okay? You know how it is with midterms coming up."

He should. It was the end of October, and he should be concentrating on midterms himself. Instead, he couldn't think about anything except Simone. "If your course load is too heavy," he began, but she laughed and shook her head.

"I'm fine, I tell you. There's no reason to report me to the administration."

He'd forgotten all about reporting her to the administration. "I'm not going to report you." After arguing with himself for a week and a half, he'd finally decided to at least explore the possibility of following his father's suggestion, provided that she was even interested, of course. "It occurred to me that you might be able to get a faculty job."

She brightened instantly. "Oh?"

"That is, if you're open to it and if the right position becomes available. And if you think you can handle it."

Nodding enthusiastically, she said, "Yes, I'm definitely open to it, and I'm sure I can handle it. Unless…would I have to give up the mission?"

His frown deepened. "I'm not sure you're up to maintaining both positions."

"I'm up to it," she declared. "In fact, I'm one hundred percent certain I'd be better for it."

He wasn't so sure about that, but he supposed that was a battle they could fight later. "Well…perhaps if you put back on the weight you've lost," he suggested.

"I'll try," she promised, biting her lip.

"All right. I'll see what positions might be available."

"Thank you," she gushed, reaching out to clasp his forearm with her long, slender fingers.

Just that little touch made his breath hitch, and he covered her hand with his to maintain the contact, pointing out, "No one's come up with a job offer yet, Simone."

Her smile melted him. "I meant, thank you for looking out for me."

"Sure."

The fact was he couldn't help himself. Looking out for her seemed to have become second nature for him. It was more than that, though. He couldn't get through a day anymore without seeing her. He seemed to find some excuse to catch a glimpse of her and have a word at least in passing, even if he had to drop by the mission to accomplish it. He'd given up going by Chatam House. She was never there, apparently, except to shower and sleep. Lately they never seemed to have a private moment, and he found that he missed her terribly. Why else would he track her down like this on a Tuesday when he could have waited one more day and spoken to her after class?

Had it really been almost two months since she'd dropped into his arms like a cut flower at the graduate student mixer? In that time, she'd somehow firmly fixed herself in his life, and he was all too aware that he couldn't say the same in reverse. In that respect, it was Brigitte all over again. The comparison chilled him, for Brigitte had died all too young.

The fact that Simone had gained weight and then lost at least some of it again suddenly terrified him. He stood there with a lump in his throat, watching her get into the car, *his* car, and drive away, while he prayed that she was truly well.

Oh, Lord, don't let me lose her, he begged. And she wasn't even his to lose. Not even close to being his. And she really shouldn't be, but here he was trying to get her on staff just in case they might have a chance at…something.

He felt as stupid and dreamy and confused as the most inexperienced freshman boy with a hopeless crush on the senior head cheerleader—and with about as much chance of making it work between them.

Only maturity and sheer grit helped him keep his distance for the remainder of the week. He vowed that he would content himself with mere nods and casual greetings when Simone entered and left the lecture hall. The fact that he had nothing whatsoever to offer on the faculty-job front grated, but he had feelers out in all the right places, and whenever something came up, he would be among the very first to know. The rest was in God's hands.

He congratulated himself on his self-control too soon, however, for he had barely walked into his office suite midafternoon on Thursday when his administrative assistant, Vicki, informed him that he was wanted at Chatam House immediately. He dug out his cell phone, which he had forgotten to take off silent, and saw that he had a message from Chatam House. For the aunties, at his "earliest convenience" was urgent; "immediately" could only be dire, and dire, to his mind, could only pertain to Simone.

Tearing out of the building at a run, he broke all traffic laws on the short trip across town, praying as he went. Vicki, bless her, had apparently called ahead to let them know that he was on his way, for Hypatia met him in the foyer, uncharacteristically wringing her hands.

"What's happened? What's wrong? Is Brooks here?"

"Brooks? Why on earth would we call a doctor? Asher, perhaps, if Chester had his way," she grumbled.

Asher? But his cousin Asher was a lawyer. This made no sense at all.

Before he could ask another question, Hypatia led him straight into the large formal parlor, where Simone sat alone upon the antique brocade settee and everyone else—Magnolia, Odelia, Kent, Chester, Hilda and now Morgan and Hypatia—stood, arranged around the low piecrust tea table like an inquisition panel. Simone glanced up at him, and he could not mistake the stubborn tilt of her sweetly pointed little chin. He almost smiled in relief. Whatever was going on, she wasn't ill, but then that begged the question…

"What is this about?"

Chester pointed an accusatory finger. "She's stealing food."

Now that was the last problem with which Morgan had expected to be presented, but he did note that Simone ducked her head. "What?"

"Stealing!" Chester all but shouted, and Simone sighed. "And no small amount. Enough to feed two people at least."

"That's preposterous," Morgan said, almost chuckling. "She couldn't possibly be stealing food. Whatever for, when she's welcome to anything she could want? Besides, she's obviously not eating it." She rolled a murderous glare up at him, arms folded. "Well, look at her," he insisted. "She's losing weight, not gaining."

Odelia cleared her throat, reminding him that it was impolite to discuss a lady's weight. Morgan mentally sighed. It wasn't his plump auntie's weight in question. She wasn't being accused of stealing food. Suddenly it hit him, and he did chuckle.

"I know what this is about. I told Simone that she

needed to regain the weight that she'd recently lost as a sort of condition for my helping her get a faculty job at BCBC."

"So she started stealing whole casseroles and pork tenderloins?" Chester countered. "I caught her red-handed." He pointed to a cardboard box on a rectangular chinoiserie table beside the open pocket doorway. "She boxed it up while Hilda was in the laundry. Took it right out of the refrigerator and boxed it up to cart it out, and it wasn't the first time, either. We've been missing foodstuffs out of the pantry and refrigerator for more than a week."

Morgan hadn't recovered from the shock of that before Chester hurried on, exclaiming, "And that isn't the whole of it. There's been something fishy from the beginning. She all but hides herself. You sisters, you think she doesn't want to impose, but the girl won't even look a body in the eye, and there's the coming and going at all hours, when it's not like she's got a fella or friends to go around with. It's not that at all. I don't know what it is, but something isn't right, and it's been eating at me since she come here."

It was eating at Morgan, too, now, gnawing a hole right through his middle. He'd noticed that she didn't like to *be* at Chatam House, when everyone else who'd ever stayed there had fallen in love with the place and its occupants, and that business about not letting Chester drive her around bothered him. Morgan was still at a loss to explain her complete animosity to the idea when she'd accepted the much larger favor of the loan of a car from him. He wanted to think that it was simply because the car belonged to him, but she'd gone so far as to resort to an inconvenient, and dangerous, moped rather than accept the transportation generously offered to her by the aunties and Chester. Something just didn't add up.

Like everyone else in the room, he looked to Simone for some sort of answer, an easy, simple explanation. Dozens could be found, surely. She had but to supply one or two, and this would all be over, but she sat like a guilty lump, her eyes downcast, until suddenly she shot to her feet.

"I'm moving out," she proclaimed shakily. "Now."

Just like that, she dashed his every hope for a reasonable explanation, and just like that something popped into his mind, something he had dismissed and shouldn't have, something he knew and no one else here did, a question that had to be asked. Instinctively, he knew that she wouldn't be the one to give him the answer, however, so he asked the one person who might.

"Who is Laverne Davenport Worth?"

Simone gasped and dropped back onto the settee as if she'd been felled with a blow. Chester first looked confused then stunned. A moment passed before he formulated the answer.

"She is my mother."

Simone made a small, strangling sound.

"And she lives in Fort Worth," Morgan surmised, shaking his head, for it still made no sense to him.

"In a nursing home there," Chester supplied. "She is in a vegetative coma and has been for a dozen years or more. She was in an accident."

Morgan shifted to face Simone. His feet felt like lead weights, and his heart literally trembled in his chest, for if nothing else, he knew he was about to brand her a liar. "Why did you list her as your next of kin on your admissions application?"

For a long, tense moment, he thought Simone wouldn't answer, but then she shook her head, her lips twisting, and in a voice barely above a whisper said, "It was the only address I could verify without…"

"Without?" he prodded.

She looked up, her enormous, storm-gray eyes brimming with tears and apology. "Without giving myself away prematurely." Looking to Chester then, she whispered, "Uncle Chester, I'm so sorry."

The portly man stumbled back and came down hard on the striped occasional chair in front of the fireplace. "Lyla!" he gasped.

Just that one word brought a shriek from Hilda, who clapped chubby hands to flaccid cheeks, bawling, "Lyla Simone! I don't believe it. It is you! But why not just say so? What were you thinking?"

Lyla Simone? Morgan felt as if he was reeling, though his feet were firmly planted.

"Carissa's Lyla?" he heard someone ask.

"Phillip's Carissa?"

"*Our* Carissa?"

Carissa's sister. His cousin Phillip's sister-in-law. Morgan thought he would drop where he stood.

"I thought she was missing."

"She *was* missing."

"Ran away as a girl."

"It nearly killed your daddy," Chester accused. "Why didn't you come back before he died?"

"I shouldn't have come back at all!" Simone bolted up from the sofa and ran for the door. "Don't tell Carissa. Please don't!"

"Don't tell her?" Chester demanded, coming to his feet. "That's daft."

Openly sobbing, Simone grabbed the box of food and dashed into the foyer.

"Now where is she off to?" Chester demanded.

"I'm not sure," Morgan said, still too stunned to move, "but I do know why she didn't come home during her father's illness." Whatever else might be lies, the cancer was truth.

"Left it to her sister to care for their dying daddy," Chester accused, throwing out a hand. "That's Lyla's way."

Morgan looked to Hypatia in exasperation. This was clearly a Worth family matter, and he didn't know the intricacies of it, but he did know where Simone, or Lyla, had been and what she had been doing for at least eighteen months of her father's illness. "Didn't you tell them what we found out?"

Hypatia shook her head morosely. "I wasn't aware of the connection and felt she was entitled to her privacy."

Her *secrecy,* more like. Well, they'd all had enough of that. He faced Chester squarely and put it to him. "She didn't come home before her father died because she was too busy fighting for her own life. She's had cancer and just barely beat it, if I'm any judge."

The older man turned pale, from the crown of his shiny bald pate to the tips of his puffy fingers. "Oh, no. You're sure about that?"

"Very."

"It's why she's here, Chester," Hypatia supplied. "Brooks insisted that she have a safe, quiet place in which to recover."

Chester heaved out a great breath. "Well, that doesn't explain the last decade, but it's something." He glanced around at them, demanding, "So, what are we standing here for? We have to go after her."

"That we do," Morgan agreed grimly, striding after her. Chester fell in behind him.

"Wait for me!" Hypatia called, springing after them.

Morgan paused only long enough to see her through the front door. The coupe had already turned onto the street and was heading west.

"She's getting away," Hypatia complained, trotting across the porch and down the steps.

"I may know where's she's going," Morgan said, leaving it to Chester to put his aunt into the passenger seat of the BMW. "At least I think we should start looking at the mission. You'll have to take another vehicle, Chester."

"No problem, sir."

Hypatia filled him in on the Worth situation as he drove, trying mightily to keep the coupe in sight, without success. It chilled him to the bone to think of Simone running away from home when she was barely even old enough to drive a car. Only God knew how she'd managed to keep body and soul together in the intervening years. He wanted to shake her and hold her at the same time, and his greatest fear was that she would take off again, just disappear from all their lives.

To think that she was Chester Worth's niece and his own cousin Phillip's sister-in-law and living right under their noses for two whole months, thanks to him, amazed him. No wonder she hadn't wanted to move into Chatam House and wouldn't let Chester drive her around town. She was afraid of being found out. The mystery was why Chester hadn't recognized her on sight. Morgan supposed she had changed. What the passing years and maturity hadn't done, the cancer probably had. But why was she intent on hiding her identity?

A lump began to grow in the center of Morgan's chest, a great black mass of fear and doubt. What had she done that she couldn't bear for her family to know about? He wasn't sure that he wanted to know himself, yet he couldn't deny the relief he felt when he saw the coupe in the parking lot at the mission.

"Dad's car isn't here, so she probably locked the door behind her," he said. "I'll go see, and if it's locked, I'll try around back."

"You don't think she'll let us in?" Hypatia asked as he exited the vehicle.

"No, I don't. Wait here for Chester. If I can't get in, I'll call Dad to come down."

Her lips set in a grim line, Hypatia nodded. Morgan jogged up the concrete steps to the front door and tried the knob. Locked tight, just as expected. Shaking his head at Hypatia, he went down the steps and loped around the building to the back, where a deck had been built behind a chain-link fence next to the rail yard. He took the back steps in one long stride and crept across the deck to the door there. It thankfully yielded to the touch.

Letting out a breath of relief, he walked inside, finding only gloom at first. The long interior hallway that neatly bisected the building into two unequal sides definitely could use more lighting. He walked along the polished concrete floor, feeling the heavy silence, toward the main rooms. Then he heard it, a soft female voice coming from behind a simple door.

"It's all right. Don't cry."

A sniff, then, "No. No, it's not. I promised to take care of you, and I've messed up everything."

Morgan tilted his head, recognizing Simone's voice. He didn't know who was with her, but whoever she was, he suspected that she was the reason for the food theft and perhaps for much else. Reaching out, he quietly turned the knob and let the door swing open on a small, stringently clean, plainly furnished room.

Inside was a twin bed with a small shelf and lamp fixed to the wall next to it. He could see a tiny bathroom, a cubbyhole for hanging clothes with a single drawer beneath it and a braided rug on the floor. Posters of outdoor scenes with Bible verses printed on them had been mounted on the walls, but that was it for decoration. Simone and Rina sat side by side on the rumpled bed.

Simone immediately came to her feet, taking up a spot between him and the girl, trying to block his view—but not, however, before he had seen what she would have hidden. The oversize sweater that Rina normally wore hung from the rod in the cubbyhole, leaving her clad in a form-fitting tank top that exposed all too clearly the swollen belly of a very pregnant teenager.

Everything clicked into place: Rina's stubborn refusals to ride anything requiring restraints at the amusement park, the oversize clothes, her apparent girth despite her tiny hands and feet, the many trips to the bathroom. This, undoubtedly, was one of the two emergency rooms reserved for Child Protective Services to use when they couldn't immediately place a foster child who had come unexpectedly into their care through the mission. He saw as well the faded bruises on Rina's throat, arms and face. What he didn't already know, he simply asked of Simone, his heart already swelling with pride and understanding.

"How long have you been hiding her and from whom?"

"He beat her," Simone said, looking at Rina, now clad once more in the gargantuan sweater that she hid beneath. "He tried to make her get an abortion, and when that didn't work, he beat her to try to make her lose the baby."

"What a horrible thing," Hypatia remarked.

Simone nodded and went on. "Her family can't take her in, and she doesn't dare go to a local shelter for fear he'll find her. She doesn't have money to go anywhere else. All I could think to do was hide her here."

"And try to feed her," Morgan surmised, glancing at Chester, who had the grace to blush.

"You might have come to me," Hypatia said kindly, but Simone shook her head, willing back the tears.

"I couldn't do that," she whispered, "not after all

you've already done, not after my own—" she swallowed hard and forced out the word "—deception. But I suppose what I've done was worse."

Hypatia clucked her tongue and patted Simone's shoulder. "Perhaps you didn't use the best judgment, but you did what you thought was best. As for the other, well, you left out a few things, but we'll get to them."

That was very much what Simone feared. Glumly, she nodded.

"Now," Hypatia said briskly, addressing herself to Rina, "as for you, young lady, we can certainly accommodate you at Chatam House for as long as you need."

"Huh?" Rina looked up, as wide-eyed as a deer caught in headlights.

"You'll be safe and comfortable there, I promise you," Hypatia went on, "and you won't have to hide. My nephew Asher is an attorney, and he will see that you and your child are legally protected."

Rina looked appalled. "Ma'am, I can't afford no attorney."

Hypatia waved that away as inconsequential. "You leave that to the Chatams."

"But, ma'am—"

"It's miss," Chester interrupted, not unkindly. "Miss Chatam will take care of everything, don't you fear." He reached down to help the girl to her feet. "You come along now. We can fix you up a nice place in the carriage house."

Simone instantly saw red. Outraged on Rina's behalf, she spoke without thinking. "Are you saying she's not good enough to stay in the mansion, Uncle Chester?"

He recoiled as if she'd slapped him. "Not at all. I only thought she might be uncomfortable in the—"

"Mansion!" Rina squawked, drawing back. "I ain't going to no *mansion*. What would I do in a fancy place? I'd rather stay here."

"No, no, it's not like that," Simone assured her. "It's…" Gilded, filled with priceless antiques, enormous. Even she felt overawed and out of place there, despite the kindness of the Chatams. She slipped an arm around the girl's quaking shoulders. "It's all right, truly, but if you'll be more comfortable in the carriage house, that's fine."

Morgan stepped in then and set things to right. "Rina, you go with Chester. He will get you settled in wherever you're most comfortable. Simone will check on you soon."

Simone nodded encouragingly, and Rina let Chester lead her from the room, but then, just before they slipped through the door, Simone had to speak up. "Uncle Chester, please, about Carissa. Don't call her. Not yet."

He made an exasperated sound, nodded and led Rina from the room. Simone tried to feel relief. At least Rina and her baby would be safe and well cared for by the Chatams. She had no doubt that they would help the girl establish herself somehow. Rina had spoken lately of giving the baby up for adoption, and perhaps that was for the best. So many deserving couples who could not conceive yearned for children to love. She turned off that thought, telling herself that she had bigger problems to face just now, imminent ones.

Hypatia turned to Simone and asked what she had been dreading, what she knew was coming.

"Why don't you want your sister to know you're here?"

Simone gulped down the big doughy knot in her throat and tried to get in a breath so she could explain. "I thought I would come home to my father." Tears welled, tears to which she was not entitled, and she bowed her head to hide them. "He was a good man, my dad. For a while, I was too ashamed to come back and face him, but during my illness I was led to true salvation by a hospital chaplain, and I thought… I *hoped* that if I confessed everything to my dad, he would forgive me and gradually the rest of the family would forgive me, too."

"I'm sure that's true," Hypatia told her. "What I know of your father leads me to believe that he would have forgiven wholeheartedly."

Simone smiled in bittersweet confirmation. "But it's too late for that. Too late for everything. And I just have to go on from here somehow, have to do the best I can with what I have left. Isn't that what God expects of me, Miss Hypatia?" she asked. "He spared my life. The rest I deserve. Shouldn't I do the best I can with what He's left me?"

"Child, I do not know what you're saying," Hypatia admitted.

"The contempt of my family," Simone gritted out, "childlessness, being alone, I deserve that. But shouldn't I do the best I can with what's left to me? Isn't that what God expects of me? That's all I'm trying to do. That's all I want to do."

"Why on earth would you think yourself deserving of contempt?" Morgan asked. "You're not making sense."

Simone carefully wrapped her arms around herself, feeling as brittle and insubstantial as spun glass now that the time for full disclosure had come. "Don't you see?" she asked mechanically. "I am Rina. I was her. Not even seventeen and pregnant. Only I wasn't smart enough to run from my boyfriend. He beat me until my baby died."

Chapter Ten

Her legs collapsed unexpectedly. Fortunately, Simone stood close enough to the bed to land on its edge. Hypatia yelped, but Morgan reached her first. She held him off with stiff arms, knowing that if he touched her, she'd give way to the grief that she had buried for so long. It hovered around her now, ready to pounce like a ravenous animal. She had miscarried a tiny baby and had it swept away like so much garbage with no doctor or medical personnel of any kind ever attending her.

"That was just the beginning," she forged on, her vision narrowing to a foggy pinprick. "He kept me in that same room for weeks, and he told me that he owed money to some men and I had to work it off for him." She closed her eyes, feeling dizzy. "I was such an idiot. I thought he was helping the other girls there. I didn't know they were prostitutes until he told me."

She heard Hypatia's gasp then, and her vision snapped back into focus. There it was, the revulsion and horror, everything she'd expected to see, everything she'd always felt.

"I was fortunate," she went on woodenly. "The police came before the men did. They arrested me with the others, but I didn't care. He'd gotten me a fake ID." She laughed harshly. "I thought that was *so* cool. At least my record is under the wrong name, and the cops didn't know how young I was, so my family didn't have to know how low I'd sunk. I lived on the street and ate out of garbage cans until after my seventeenth birthday so they wouldn't know."

"Oh, Simone," Hypatia said, "your father would have been happy to have you home under any circumstances."

"I realize that now," she admitted, "now that it's too late. But what of my mother?"

Hypatia blanched and looked away.

"I see you've met my mother," Simone said wryly, "and you must know my sister quite well, too."

"I like to think so."

"Responsible, upright, persistent and hardworking, honest to a fault, makes do without complaining, never puts a foot wrong?"

Hypatia smiled. "She is."

"If you were her, wouldn't you resent me?" Simone asked.

Hypatia opened her mouth, blinked and sighed.

"She has children now and a happy marriage," Simone went on. "What could I possibly add to her life but regret and shame? She can't want that."

"You're her sister," Hypatia said simply.

"Not for a long time," Simone murmured, sinking down onto the bed. "Just let me rest a little while please."

A hand skated beneath her bangs to cover her forehead, and she heard Morgan say, "She's as cold and clammy as a fish."

That was exactly how she felt, Simone thought, curling into a ball, like a fish out of water. She wanted to sleep and never wake up again. Tears leaked from her shuttered eyes.

"I'm taking her to Brooks," Morgan stated.

It sounded to Simone as if she was at the bottom of a deep well.

"Lyla Simone," Hypatia called down to her, "Morgan will look after you, dear."

Morgan, she thought. What would she do, where would she go, how would she survive without Morgan, she wondered, and how soon would she have to find out?

"Obviously she's been skipping meals," Morgan pointed out.

Brooks shot him a speaking glance. A blind man could tell that she'd lost weight recently, but Morgan had felt that someone should clearly state the cause.

Thursday was a half day at the clinic, but Brooks had met them there, and Morgan was extremely grateful. Not grateful enough, however, to take the hint and leave the examining room when Brooks glanced pointedly at the door and nodded in that direction.

"Don't even try it," Morgan told him, folding his arms.

Brooks looked to Simone, but she just shrugged, so Morgan stayed put.

"As I told you over the phone, she's cold to the touch but seems to be perspiring, and her pulse is rapid."

"I'm just tired," Simone murmured.

"Are you getting plenty of rest?" Brooks asked, checking her pulse himself.

"Yes."

"Then are you taking your supplements?"

She looked away.

"What supplements?" Morgan asked.

"I wrote a prescription for her," Brooks said pointedly, reaching for the blood pressure cuff.

Seated on the end of the examination table, Simone leaned forward and looked down at her toes, her hands in her lap. Taking up a position directly in front of her, Morgan willed her to look at him while Brooks wrapped the cuff around her upper arm and pumped it tight with the squeeze ball in his hand.

"Pressure's a little low," he announced after a minute or so, then he turned to the computer terminal to record his findings.

Morgan bent forward at the waist, trying to capture Simone's gaze, and pointedly asked, "Did you even fill the prescription?"

She made a face, and that was all the answer he needed.

"Honestly, Simone!" he scolded.

"Do you know how much those pills cost?" she shot back. "Nearly two weeks' pay!" She tossed a hand at Brooks, adding, "He said I'd get over the anemia eventually, anyway."

Brooks looked around warily. "That's true," he agreed. "I even warned her not to follow the iron-rich diet longer than—"

"Iron-rich diet!" Morgan interrupted hotly. "Does she look like she's been on an iron-rich diet to you?"

"When people are giving you free room and board, you don't demand special diets, too," Simone said defensively.

Brooks spread his hands. "Have you done anything I prescribed?"

"I've been at Chatam House all this time, haven't I?"

"Well, that's something, I suppose," Brooks said drily, but Morgan shook his head.

"I do not understand how your mind works," he told her. "You will steal food for a pregnant friend, but you won't ask for what you need from people who are willing, *eager,* to help you. What is that? A death wish?"

"No."

"What, then?" he demanded.

"I don't know! I just didn't want to put anyone out. I just…" She looked down.

She just thought she wasn't worth it. He didn't have to hear her say it to know it, and the very idea infuriated, appalled and broke him into little pieces inside.

"Now, you listen to me," he told her, shaking his finger in her face. "You are going to get well. In every sense of the word, you are going to *heal* completely. No matter if I have to…" What? Tie her down and shove pills into her? Force-feed her? Open her head and pluck out every silly notion there? Love her until she believed she was worth it?

But he already loved her. He couldn't help loving her. He loved her against his own will. And it hadn't made a bit of difference. How could it?

Shaken, he ran a hand through his hair and turned on Brooks.

"What now?"

"Feed her a steak and a spinach salad," Brooks said. "Then take her home and put her to bed. I'll send around the prescription and a diet plan tomorrow."

"Done," Morgan said, daring her to argue.

"You might try lightening up on the emotional drama," Brooks added almost flippantly.

"I would if I could," Morgan returned in kind.

"Wouldn't we all?" Simone sighed, sliding down off the table. "God knows I did everything I could to avoid it."

And she had, he realized. She really had.

"It'll be all right," he promised her with all sincerity, because it had to be. For once, something had to be all right for her. *Please, God,* he prayed.

He drove her straight to a little French bistro in town. There they had beef tips in a rich brown sauce, French onion soup and spinach salad, followed by strawberries Romanoff. She ate heartily and thanked him with a smile, but when they were back in the car, tears started to roll.

"I don't want to go back to Chatam House. I can't face them there. Couldn't I go back to the boarding-house?"

"Even if they still had a room for you, which is doubtful," he pointed out, "you know you wouldn't rest there."

"The mission, then, just for tonight."

He shook his head. "I don't like the idea of you being alone there, especially at night. Be honest now. Were you comfortable with the thought of Rina being there alone at night?"

Reluctantly, she shook her head.

Morgan thought a moment. He could always put

her up in a motel, but that wouldn't look great if it ever came to light, and as much as he hated to admit it, he couldn't be entirely sure now that she would be there when morning came. His aunts were not the only ones with room to spare, however.

"I suppose I could call my dad."

Simone winced. "I guess he'll have to know eventually, but…"

"Sweetheart, you're the only one condemning you. Your uncle and aunt are just…hurt and confused right now, but that will pass, if it hasn't already."

"You're just saying that."

He searched for a way to convince her, but she was her own best proof. "Simone, what did you do after you turned seventeen? How did you get off the street?"

She swiped at her tears with her fingertips. "Well, one of the shelters offered GED classes, so I got my high school diploma that way."

"Then you went to college."

"Junior college first."

"You must have had a job."

"Several," she said drily.

"So you went to work and put yourself through college," he summarized, "and all that time you kept your nose clean."

"I didn't dare risk—"

"You stayed out of trouble," he interrupted firmly,

"you worked, you went to school, all on your own, alone, as a teenager, without any help from anyone."

She licked her lips. "Yes. All right."

"And eventually you found someone and got married. He turned out to be a creep…"

"Story of my life," she muttered.

"But at least he was a wealthy creep," Morgan went on, and at last she smiled.

"Well, yes, there is that."

"So now your schooling is entirely paid for."

"And that is a blessing for which I am deeply grateful," she said sincerely.

"Look, you've made mistakes," he told her. "Everyone does."

"Not like mine," she argued.

"And you've paid for them," he insisted. "You've overcome heartaches and obstacles that would have broken lesser women, Simone, and you have a great many accomplishments of which you should be proud. Give yourself some credit. Don't always expect the worst. You might be surprised."

She seemed to consider that, but then she slanted a glance up at him and said, "You've never met my mother, have you?"

He chuckled. "Can't say I've had the pleasure."

Simone smiled, but her eyes remained sad. "If you had, you might understand when I say that my apple didn't fall very far from her tree."

"Now you're just being silly," he told her. "You're

arguing a genetics hypothesis, when I know perfectly well that I'm sitting here looking at a self-made woman if ever there was one."

"But that's the point, Morgan," she said gently. "I made myself a pariah in my own family."

He shook his head. "I'll believe that when I see it."

"I'm afraid you will," she told him sadly.

He gusted a great sigh and shook his head at her. "So what's it to be, then?" he asked. "Do you run again, or do you stay and face the music?"

"Are those really the only two choices?" she asked, her voice an agony of hope.

"That's how I see it," he answered forthrightly. "The thing is, if you run, you'll be alone again, but if you stay…" He held out his hand.

Gulping, she laid her palm against his. "Chatam House, then. And pray for time, I suppose."

"Simone," he began, curling his fingers around hers, but then he paused. "Should I go on calling you Simone?"

"I've been Simone so long now I don't know how to be Lyla anymore," she told him.

"Simone," he began again, "time works both ways. Give your family some time. They'll come around."

"I hope so," she said, "but you can't really understand, because you're a Chatam."

Maybe you could be, too, he thought, squeezing her hand. But no, she needed a younger man, a man with the time to be approved for adoption. It was too late for him. Like she'd said, it was just too late for some things.

"You need some rest," he said, shifting in his seat and releasing her hand to start up the car engine. "It's been a trying day."

The day had faded, however, until nothing of the sun could even be seen along the horizon as they drove west toward Chatam House from the bistro. Night would soon envelop the day entirely.

He got out and went around to help her out of the low-slung car. They walked up the brick path side by side and climbed the steps to the porch. Crossing that deep veranda in silence, they came to the bright yellow door that marked Chatam House as one of the sunniest places on earth—for everyone but her, he supposed. Morgan simply opened the door and held it wide for her to walk through. She did so with marked reluctance, her hands clasped behind her. He followed her to the foot of the stairs.

"I'll bring the coupe over for you later tonight," he promised. He'd get a buddy to help. Someone was always willing to drive his Beemer for him.

One foot on the bottom step, one hand on the gracefully curving banister, Simone closed her eyes, clearly having forgotten that they'd left the coupe at the mission. "Seems I am forever in your debt."

"You're never in my debt," he told her, squeezing the hand that hung at her side. "Now, get some rest."

Nodding, she began the climb. He watched her

until she turned out of sight, then he went in search of his aunts. Odelia's husband was a pharmacist by trade. Simone would have the rest, diet and prescription she needed, or someone—everyone—would answer to Morgan Chatam.

Morgan's surprise and pleasure when she turned up for class the next day couldn't have been more evident, but Simone would much rather have been at the university than Chatam House, where her uncle and aunt tried to convince her to call her sister and the Chatams asked how she was feeling every time they saw her. She couldn't even check on Rina without someone checking on her. At least the Chatams called her Lyla Simone, using both names, while her uncle and aunt insisted on calling her Lyla. She wanted to snap at them that Lyla was an idiot child, while Simone was a woman, but they had reluctantly agreed to delay informing Carissa of her presence for the time being, so she said nothing. In truth, she was both—the child who still suffered for her mistakes and the woman who paid for them. She was only too happy to escape to class when the opportunity came.

"You look good," Morgan said by way of greeting when she first came into the lecture hall. Some of the girls around them tittered, so he immediately amended the statement. "*Well,* I mean. You look *well.* How are you feeling?"

"I'm quite recovered," she said. "Thank you."

Then for good measure, she added, "Dr. Leland has taken good care of me."

Morgan nodded and grinned. "I always recommend Dr. Leland."

"I can see why," she murmured, heading for her seat.

"Uh, stop by my desk after class, Simone," Morgan called. "I want to talk to you about that staff position we discussed."

She shot him a surprised look and a curt nod before hurrying on her way. She hoped that was good news. Surely he wasn't going to withdraw his recommendation. As she took her seat, she heard the two students in front of her whispering.

"A staff position? How did she swing that?"

"She's a graduate student picking up a prerequisite."

"Oh. Slumming, eh?"

Stung, Simone bent toward them and hissed, "You don't know what slumming is until you've lived on the street and eaten out of garbage cans."

To her surprise, they did not recoil. Instead, they turned in their seats to face her.

"Did you really?" the young man asked. "Live on the street, I mean."

Simone dropped her gaze, wishing she'd kept her mouth shut. She didn't want to lie, though. She had tried so hard not to lie throughout all this, though some would say she was merely playing at semantics. Well, no more. Finally, she gave a brief nod.

"Wow," he said, "what a testimony you must have."

She jerked her gaze up. Was he serious? "T-testimony?"

"Look at you now, a graduate student in Bible college."

"God must have done a real work in your life," the girl surmised, her smile warm and accepting.

A work in her life? Through homelessness and cancer?

The boy pulled a card from a pocket and pressed it into Simone's hand, saying, "We're always looking for people to speak to our group, if you're interested and have the time."

Speak to a group? Simone didn't know what to say to that. "I—I'm pretty busy." For good measure, she added, "I work part-time at the DBC mission for youth and young adults over next to the rail yard."

"Yeah? That sounds interesting," the girl said. "What's it like?"

Simone relaxed, and they discussed the mission for several minutes until Morgan started class. Afterward, the young man rose to his feet and smiled down at Simone, suggesting, "Hey, maybe our group could come over to the mission sometime, and you could talk to us there."

Once again, Simone didn't know what to say. "Uh, maybe. I'll…see what the director thinks about that."

"We'll pray about it," the girl said, getting up.

"Cool deal," the guy called, starting off. The girl followed.

Simone blinked at them, wondering what had just happened. Could she really tell her story to a bunch of kids? She would die of embarrassment and shame.

Then again, if just one of them learned something from it…

She shook her head. No, no, not these kids. These kids didn't need to learn from her. They had it together. They were in Bible college, leading good, pure lives. No, the kids who needed to hear what she had to say were the kids at the mission. But did she dare? She bit her lip, pondering the matter as the room emptied. Eventually, she stood, packed her wheeled case and made her way to Morgan.

He handed her a sheaf of papers. "The job is in the Records Department. Work from home, make your own hours. It's mostly typing. Fill-in-the-blank sort of stuff. Entry-level. I'm told it's a good department to get into because every department has records. Even the Records Department has its own records. It's administrative, not academic, but it gets you on staff, and that's what I'm—" He broke off, huffed and said, "Maybe it's not what you're after."

"No, it sounds fine," she told him. "In fact, it sounds great."

"The pay isn't stellar," he warned, "but it's far above what you're earning now."

She thumbed through to that section of the paper-work and literally gaped at the salary offered. "That's fantastic! Oh, my."

"Okay, then. The top sheet there tells you how to go online and fill out the application."

"I'll do it right away," she promised, smiling broadly.

"You do that, and I'll pray," he said.

Touched, she tilted her head. "Thank you, Morgan."

"No, not this time," he refuted, shaking his head. "This time, I honestly don't know if I'm doing the right thing."

"Of course you are."

"I don't know," he told her. "I just really don't know."

She knew that he was worried about her health. "I'm fine. Truly. And what isn't fine is my own fault, not yours."

"That isn't what I mean," he said. "My motives may not always be as pure as you think."

She lifted her hand to his cheek, whispering, "One thing I know about you, Morgan Chatam, is that you always do the right thing."

"I hope so," he replied softly, blanketing her hand with his. "I pray so."

He didn't sleep well.

And that, Morgan told himself blearily the next morning, *is what comes of a guilty conscience.*

Simone didn't even realize that he'd maneuvered her into a staff position for his own purposes or why, and it did no good to tell himself that it was for her benefit when he knew his own motives. If she was on staff at the university, he could openly date her— even if he had no business doing so. Okay, so it was an easy job and she'd make more money, a lot more money; that didn't change why he'd done it.

Repeatedly throughout the night, he had told himself, and God, that he wouldn't take advantage of the situation. He wouldn't spend time with her just because he could, wouldn't take her out, wouldn't do all the little romantic things that kept popping into his head, and he definitely wouldn't hold and kiss her. The problem was that he didn't believe it, for as wrong as he knew he was for her, he wanted her with a desperation that frightened him.

For the first time in his life, he was afraid. Not angry or hurt, as he had been when Brigitte had broken their engagement. Not grief stricken and broken, as he had been when those he loved had died. Not ashamed and contrite, as he had been when he'd realized what a fool he'd made of himself after Brigitte and Brooks had married. He was afraid that his life would never be the same again because his heart would never be the same again, and he honestly was not sure that he could ever truly be happy without Simone. For whom he was all wrong.

Perhaps if she could bear a child… He couldn't

believe that he was even thinking about that at his age, but no one could tell him that he wasn't allowed to start a family the natural way; they could, however, when it came to adoption. He'd known one couple turned down several times by different agencies precisely because of age, so he'd done a little research, and what he'd found hadn't helped. Simone's health history was already a strike against her when it came to adoption through normal channels; she didn't need to add a middle-aged husband to the equation. Funny, he'd never thought of himself as middle-aged before.

Private adoption was fraught with difficulties, from scams to women who simply changed their minds and too many couples who couldn't qualify through normal channels. No, he was a strike against her, no matter how he looked at it, so he prayed that God would take this desire, this obsession, from him. It hadn't helped at all. He didn't understand. His house felt foreign now, the same house that he'd loved and treasured as his haven all these years. This neat, orderly, clean, spacious bachelor's paradise suddenly seemed sterile, cold and empty as he sat at the bar in his gourmet kitchen with a mug of coffee in hand, his glasses perched on his nose and his Bible open before him, reading aloud from Proverbs 3.

"'Trust in the Lord with all your heart, and do not rely on your own understanding.'"

Setting aside his coffee, he tossed the glasses and

dropped his head into his hands. He was trying. Oh, how he was trying.

When the phone rang, he nearly jumped off the stool. Rolling his eyes, he dug into the pocket of his terry-cloth robe and came up with the thing. Swiping his thumb across the screen, he brought it to his ear.

"Good morning."

Simone's tear-choked voice came to him through the tiny speaker. "Morgan, they called Carissa! They said they'd wait, but they've already called her, and she's coming over with her husband. Morgan, I can't do this! I can't! Not alone."

"You won't have to," he promised her, pushing back the stool. "I'll get dressed and be right over."

"Oh, Morgan. What am I going to say to her? How am I going to face her?"

"I don't know," he said, "but you won't be alone."

Not today, at least. Not so long as he could help, and not hurt, her. For now, that was all that mattered.

Chapter Eleven

For some reason, Morgan felt he should look his best. He grabbed a pair of dark brown dress slacks and a crisp white shirt, leaving the collar open and rolling up the cuffs. As a concession to the November chill, he threw a tan sweater over his shoulders, looping the sleeves across his chest. When he got to Chatam House, he found that other reinforcements had been called in; the aunties had thought it wise to have Brooks on hand. Considering the toll that the initial discovery of her true identity had taken on Simone, Morgan couldn't argue the point, but he didn't like walking in to find Brooks there dressed in a suit with only the tie missing, looking entirely too good, like he'd just come from a photo shoot for a men's fashion magazine.

Simone, too, had dressed for the occasion in a simple but expensive-looking olive-green skirt and pale pink sweater set, unadorned flats on her feet.

She wore pearls at her earlobes to match the buttons on her cardigan and a gold bangle bracelet. Sitting rigidly on the very edge of the settee, she seemed wound as tightly as an eight-day clock.

Morgan took the seat next to Simone, nodding at Brooks, who stood directly behind her. Kent overflowed the occasional chair next to Odelia's to one side of the fireplace, where a cheery blaze burned far enough back in the recess not to risk smoking the ornate white plaster front. Odelia had made a statement by covering herself in peace symbols from her earlobes to the buckles on her shoes. Hypatia, in her regal silk, and Magnolia, in a cardigan over a shirtwaist dress over a pair of trousers over muck boots, had taken the two wing chairs. Chester, meanwhile, stood sentinel beside the doorway, and Hilda bustled around the tea tray on the low piecrust table, serving everyone with forced cheer. Simone waved away the offering, but Brooks intruded on her behalf.

"If there's mint and honey for the tea, that might be calming."

"I'll get it," Hilda offered at once, scurrying away as fast as her girth would allow.

She had just returned with a small container of the prescribed additives when a faint knock came at the front door. Chester slipped out into the foyer. Muted voices could be heard conversing softly for several seconds. Then three persons stepped into the wide, open doorway. Morgan curled his hand around the inside of Simone's right wrist, her hands clasped tightly in her lap.

Both Phillip and his wife had dressed casually in corduroy jeans and hiking boots, but Phillip, who had spent years in the cool Pacific Northwest, wore only a tan T-shirt, while Carissa sported a dark green sweater. Morgan was struck immediately by the similarities between his cousin's wife and Simone. He'd only seen Carissa a few times, but he was surprised he hadn't noted their resemblance before this. She was of a height with Simone but sturdier, and her hair was longer, thicker and of a medium golden-brown color. By comparison, Simone's shorter, wispier, paler hair seemed almost red. They had the same cheekbones, however, and the same eyes, though Carissa's seemed darker and Simone's were larger and more affecting. Carissa had obviously been crying, and her tears started again when she spied her sister sitting so rigidly and silent.

Phillip slid a protective arm about his wife and glanced around the room, frowning at Brooks and lifting an eyebrow at Morgan before letting his gaze rest finally on his sister-in-law.

"She looks like Grace."

It was as if that one statement set off a bomb in the room.

"Oh, my. She does!"

"I knew there was something!"

"The hair."

"It's the eyes."

"And that chin."

"The cheeks, too."

Simone sat there frozen like a mannequin while they all stared at her and picked her apart, until Carissa spoke up, her words clipped, the tone sharp enough to eviscerate.

"Grace, in case you're wondering, is my daughter, your niece, whom you've never seen and probably didn't even know existed."

Simone dropped her gaze, but otherwise neither moved nor responded. Carissa dashed away tears and stalked deeper into the room, toward the tall, round table in the center of the floor, where Magnolia kept a large arrangement of freshly cut flowers year-round. For a moment, Morgan feared that Carissa would bump into the table and send the flowers and expensive vase flying, but she drew to a jerky halt, putting out a hand to steady herself. Phillip followed her, clasping her shoulders with his big hands. They made a striking couple, him tall and dark and ruggedly handsome, her feminine and pretty in a no-nonsense way. She didn't have Simone's ethereal elegance, though, or her wistfulness. Carissa's strength was solid, muscular; Simone's was spiritual, intelligent.

"Grace has two brothers," Carissa informed her brokenly. "Tucker is seven. Nathan is nine. You've never even held either one of them in your arms!"

"I know," Simone whispered, bowing her head. "I'm sorry."

"And to come back without a word to anyone."

"I meant to contact Dad as soon as I—"

"Well, Dad's not here!" Carissa interrupted angrily. "He died without knowing where you were or if you were all right."

"He knows now," Phillip said gently.

"That's right," Morgan agreed. "Let there be consolation in that."

But Carissa wasn't about to let her off that easily. "Where were you?" Carissa demanded.

Simone gulped. "Colorado, mostly," she answered in a rusty voice. "I knew some older kids who were going rafting there, so I went along, and I didn't come back."

"Why?" Carissa asked, obviously trying to understand.

Simone shook her head. "It was a lark at first, just something fun to do, but I knew I'd be in trouble with Dad when I got back home, and I was so tired of all the fighting, especially with Mom. It just seemed easier to be away from it. Then when things turned bad…" She took a deep breath and admitted, "I was too ashamed to come home."

Carissa narrowed her deep blue eyes at Simone and asked, "Turned bad how?"

It was the question Morgan knew Simone had

been dreading. He edged a little closer to her and felt her stiffen.

"I got involved with a pimp," she stated baldly. "He tried to put me to work for him."

It was as if all the air had been sucked out of the room. Someone, Morgan thought it was Hilda, emitted a soft little moan, but Carissa just stared at her sister mutely, as if she didn't know who or what she was. Morgan couldn't stand it.

"Tried," he said in his most authoritative tone, "is the operative word here."

To his surprise, Simone laid a quelling hand on his knee. He covered it with his own. Brooks weighed in then, swinging around the end of the settee and going down on his haunches to take Simone's left wrist between his fingers.

"I think you should rest now," he said. "You've been through enough these past few days." He looked over his shoulder at Carissa. "Your sister has suffered severe physical trauma."

Carissa turned to Chester. "I thought you said she was well."

Before Chester could speak, Brooks did. "She is well. The cancer is gone, but it takes time to regain one's strength and stamina, especially when you work as hard and suffer as many emotional blows as Simone has."

"I'm fine," Simone croaked, but it came out as dry

and crinkly as last autumn's leaves. She cleared her throat and tried again. "I'm fine."

"Nevertheless," Brooks said, "I want you to relax."

"Just one more thing," Carissa insisted. "Where did Guilland come from?"

"My husband," Simone told her. "After the marriage ended, I kept it, though I suppose legally I should go back to Worth." She looked down, adding softly, "I was going to ask Daddy's permission first."

"Well, don't ask mine," Carissa said coldly, and with that, she turned and walked out of the room.

In her wake, Simone caught her breath. Morgan squeezed her hand, but then Phillip caught his eye. Giving his head a decided yank, he let Morgan know that he wanted a word with him. Morgan didn't want to leave her, but there was Brooks practically kneeling at her feet, and Phillip might well have important information to impart.

Murmuring, "Excuse me a minute," he got up to follow his cousin into the foyer. Carissa, thankfully, was nowhere to be seen. Behind him, he heard Chester explaining that he and Hilda attended church with Phillip and Carissa.

"We couldn't very well see them there tomorrow and say nothing."

"I understand, Uncle Chester," Simone said huskily.

"At least we've broken the ice," Hilda opined cheerfully.

At that point, his aunts began urging Simone to

have some tea. Phillip, meanwhile, pulled Morgan across the foyer and practically into the library.

"Man, what are you doing mixed up in this?" he asked.

Morgan said the first words that came into his head. "Simone is my…" What? *Girlfriend? Sweetheart? Possible love?* None of those! Yet *student and friend* seemed entirely too lame a description. He started over again. "I am Simone's faculty adviser at BCBC. She's enrolled there as a graduate student. Didn't you know?"

Phillip shook his head. "No. I guess that got lost somewhere in the translation. We knew she'd been in town and here at Chatam House for a while, but not exactly why."

Morgan quickly told Phillip about the fainting and that she'd obviously been planning to reconnect with her family before she'd returned to Buffalo Creek, because she'd taken BCBC classes remotely. "She had to withdraw when she became ill, then had to make up one of my classes, which is how I wound up as her adviser. I first met her at a grad student mixer right here back in September." Thinking about that day, he snapped his fingers. "In fact, I guess I was the one to tell her about her father. I didn't know we were talking about her dad, of course. I was talking about Chester's brother passing. She must have decided then to keep her identity a secret. She is sure that with her father gone, the rest of the family won't want her."

Phillip rubbed his hand over his face. "I make no promises on that score," he said. "Carissa is plenty hurt by this, but I know my wife, and she hasn't got a mean particle in her. I'll tell you something else. She's had more than her fair share of emotional upheaval, too, but there's no quit in my girl. None."

"Simone feels terrible guilt for things she shouldn't," Morgan divulged, "and she's been through things that would have killed a lesser woman, Phillip. They're hers to tell, so I won't elaborate. I'm just saying that these Worth women must be made of some strong stuff."

Phillip straightened, looking down his princely nose at his slightly shorter and older cousin. "Is that some manly regard I hear there?"

Morgan tried to make light of it. "No. She's a student. There are rules about that sort of thing."

Phillip grinned. "Uh-huh. Never been much of one for the rules myself."

Morgan didn't know what to say to that, so he just slapped Phillip on the back and settled for a one-of-the-guys chuckle.

"Tell you what," Phillip went on. "Carissa and I will be praying about this together, and I haven't found anything so far that can't be fixed."

"Sounds like a good plan," Morgan said.

"Well, better get back to the kids. They can level

a building inside of thirty minutes." He said it with such pride that Morgan laughed.

Phillip went on his way, and when Morgan looked once more toward the parlor, he saw Brooks Leland standing in the foyer, unabashedly eavesdropping.

"Did you need something?" Morgan asked, more testily than he'd intended.

"No, I heard everything I needed to," Brooks replied smoothly.

Morgan was just about to ask what that meant when Simone appeared.

"Are they gone?"

"Yes," Morgan confirmed. "Phillip said they had to get home to the children."

She nodded stoically. "I guess I'll go up and change."

"All right." As she drew near, Morgan took her hand. "From what Phillip said, I think Carissa will come around."

"We'll see," she hedged. "At least it's over for now."

"That's right," Brooks put in. "The worst is over."

"Once my mother finds out I'm here, it will never be over," Simone said glumly.

"All the more reason for you to take it easy the rest of the day," Brooks prescribed.

Simone nodded. "I have some reading to do, anyway."

"Good. You do that," Brooks said approvingly,

"and later we'll have dinner together. How would that be?"

Morgan felt his stomach drop. Brooks and Simone having dinner together?

She glanced from Brooks to Morgan and back to Brooks again, gave a little shrug and said, "Okay. Sure."

Morgan's next breath burned like a firebrand, while Brooks stood there smirking like the cat that had eaten the canary.

"Let's make it early," he said. "I don't want you out late. So about six o'clock?"

"Fine," she said.

Then they both looked at Morgan, and what could he do but stand there, his chest so tight that it felt banded with steel? After a moment, he forced himself to speak.

"Have to get going. Lots to do."

She nodded and swiped her fingers across his cheek. "Thank you for coming."

"Always," he told her, and God help him, he meant it, even if she had just accepted a date with his best friend.

He turned and walked out of there without so much as a word of farewell for anyone.

He had never felt so betrayed or so alone. All he could think, all he could see, was Simone and Brooks.

Brooks and Simone.

Surely Brooks knew how Morgan felt about Simone—or did he? And what difference did it make? It might make all the difference, actually. Brooks was only a little younger than he, but that might be significant, and given Simone's health needs…

Yes, he told himself as he drove away from Chatam House, Brooks was definitely a better match for Simone, and now that he knew the good doctor was interested, the best thing he could do for everyone was quietly step back.

"And you always do the right thing, don't you?" he mocked himself savagely.

Simone didn't really want to go out to dinner, but she wanted to sit in her room and mope even less. If she and Morgan were going to dinner alone, she could talk freely, but it was nice of Dr. Leland to make the offer, and he had helped out that morning, more than he even knew. She wasn't certain how much more she could have taken without flying apart at the seams.

She didn't blame Carissa for being angry and resentful. Quite the contrary. That didn't make her sister's rejection and hostility any easier to bear, however.

The evening promised to be cool, so she chose to wear tweedy wool slacks, their slender legs tucked into a pair of tall leather boots, with a matching jacket and the same pink cashmere sweater from earlier in the day. She even wore her pearl earrings and the solid gold bangle with which she'd tried so mightily, and failed, to impress her sister earlier. She had come away from the Guillands with a few nice things to go along with her education, after all.

She was waiting in the foyer at precisely three minutes to six when Dr. Leland arrived, dressed just as he'd been that morning in a well-tailored brown-black suit the exact same shade as his hair and a dove-gray shirt that called attention to the distinguished spark of silver at his temples. He was a classically handsome man, very polished, with an engaging smile.

"Ah, you're ready," he said when she opened the door in answer to his knock. "Wonderful. Shall we go, then, before one of the old sweethearts catches us? I meant what I said about not keeping you out late."

Simone glanced around, but she didn't suppose she had any reason to inform anyone that she was going out, and her handbag was on her shoulder already. "Well, okay."

She slipped outside and pulled the door closed behind her. A late-model luxury sedan sat at the top of the circular drive, and he escorted her across the porch, down the steps and along the walk to it.

As they were driving away from Chatam House, she asked, "Is Morgan meeting us at the restaurant?"

The car lurched to an abrupt halt. Leland hung

his left wrist over the steering wheel and turned his head to stare at her.

"Simone, I didn't invite Morgan to dinner. I invited *you*."

Her mouth fell open. "Oh!" Oh, dear. It wasn't that she wasn't flattered—and a little irritated—it was just that she didn't want to go out with Dr. Leland. He was Morgan's best friend, and they had a history that she definitely did not want to get dragged into. "I-it's just that he was standing right there, so I assumed…"

"But that was the whole point."

"What?"

"I purposefully asked you out in front of him," the doctor explained smoothly.

She couldn't believe her ears. "*Why* would you do that?"

"I did it for him."

Now that one she had to think through, and what she came up with infuriated her. "You think I'm out to get him. You're trying to save him from my grasping clutches or some equally stupid—"

Brooks Leland put his head back and laughed until tears squeezed out the corners of his eyes.

"Sweetie," he said, "I'm doing my best to throw him straight into your arms."

She caught her breath. "Really?"

"Unless you don't want him."

"It's not that I don't want him," she said, suddenly misty-eyed, "but—"

"Buts are for billy goats," he told her, taking his foot off the brake and starting to drive. "Now, let me tell you about Morgan Chatam."

And did he ever. Over the next three hours, Dr. Leland—Brooks, as he insisted she call him—talked nonstop about his good buddy and best friend. He told Simone things that Morgan himself did not know, specifically that the woman he had loved, Brigitte, had discovered her brain tumor *before* she'd broken their engagement.

"She was a nurse," Brooks pointed out. "Knowledgeable enough to know that something wasn't right. We did the tests in secret and found the tumor right after she and Morgan got engaged."

As soon as it had been determined that the tumor was inoperable, she had broken the engagement.

"It wasn't just that she wanted to spare him," Brooks said. "We knew that we couldn't really do that. But the only treatments available at the time were even worse than the disease and with a very low success rate. She knew that he wouldn't let her rest until she'd tried everything possible, and she didn't want that."

Simone remembered Morgan saying much the same thing.

"I loved them both," Brooks went on, "so I convinced her to marry me instead. That gave me the right to make end-of-life decisions for her when she no longer could, spared Morgan the worst of it and gave Brigitte and me some good time together."

"And you're convinced it was the best possible decision for all of you?" Simone asked over a plate of grilled salmon.

"Utterly. That isn't saying it wasn't hard or that I didn't get the best end of the deal. You see, I had Brigitte, and I'd give just about anything to have a love like that again. Morgan…" Brooks pushed a sugar snap pea around on his plate with the tip of his butter knife. "I think Morgan is convinced that true love is not meant for him. Don't get me wrong. I suspect he's wild about you, completely around the bend."

Simone's heart flipped at the very notion, but she had to shake her head. "I don't know what makes you say that."

"Oh, you think that just because he's nice and conscientious with everyone that you're nothing special to him, but I know Morgan Chatam better than anyone on the planet, and I have never seen him look at another woman the way he looks at you."

Simone bit her lip. If Morgan could look at her like that after everything he knew about her, maybe he did feel something special. A terrible kind of hope filled her. Could it be?

"Of course," Brooks went on, "I've always said that Morgan is the dumbest smart guy I've ever known. The man is utterly brilliant, but I figure he's worried about your cancer returning."

"I can't blame him," Simone said, deflated. "I'm concerned about that, too. It's not fair to ask someone to invest emotionally in a person who could have a serious illness."

"You are talking to a man who married a woman he *knew* was dying," Brooks pointed out. "But, hey, we're all dying, some of us are just doing it faster than others. And some of us who are perfectly healthy get killed crossing the street. Look, God doesn't promise us tomorrow. He promises us eternity with Him. So when He hands us love in this life, we ought to grab it with both hands, no matter what. Don't you agree?"

"Yes," Simone said after a moment of thought. "Yes, I do."

"The key," Brooks told her, "is to know when it's something God has planned for you and when it's not. You see, the moment Brigitte told me she was breaking her engagement to Morgan, I knew exactly what God's plan was, but Brigitte struggled, and that's what I sense with Morgan right now. Like her, I doubt he can see past the issues to the design just yet, issues like the possibility of the cancer returning. And I suspect he may think he's too old for you."

Simone laughed dismissively. "That's silly. It never even occured to me."

"I know, but it would to Morgan because he's had

so many young girls throw themselves at him over the years." Brooks made a face and rubbed a fist against his eye. "Boo-hoo. Poor professor."

Simone laughed again. "You should hear the way they talk about him on campus. A rock star would be envious."

"Ridiculous, isn't it?" He waved a hand. "But that'll all calm down once he's married."

Married. Simone's heart skipped a beat. "You make it sound so easy, but he hasn't settled down yet."

"You've only been on the scene a couple months. You don't break a forty-five-year-long streak in a wink of an eye. Besides, you *are* a student, and that is a problem."

"I'll tell you a secret," she said softly. "I would quit school, but I'd lose a vast amount of money, enough to pay for the rest of my education. Still, it would be worth it if he really cares for me." She shook her head, not quite able to believe it.

Brooks waved a hand flippantly. "Oh, you don't have to do that. You're a grad student. All he'd have to do is get you on staff. Then the nonfraternization rules wouldn't apply."

Simone didn't realize that her jaw was swinging in the breeze until the good doctor reached across and gently pushed it back into place.

"Was it something I said?"

"More something he did," she squeaked out, gulping back the tears. "Now, if I just get the job, I guess we can assume that it's all part of God's plan for me and Morgan."

Brooks sat back and slapped the edge of the table, grinning. "Why, that sly old dog."

Chapter Twelve

Despite the tense encounter with her sister earlier in the day, Simone slept well and, thanks to her dinner with Dr. Leland, woke on Sunday morning anxious to get to church and see Morgan. He did not, sadly, seem as anxious to see her. He went out of his way to avoid her, always managing to put a long line of people between them. She wound up sitting next to his father, while Morgan sat next to his brother-in-law, who sat next to Morgan's sister, who sat on Hub's other side.

He'd have bolted up the corridor immediately after the service if Kent and Odelia hadn't gotten in his way and blocked the aisle, giving Simone enough time to work her way past Hub, Kaylie and Kaylie's rather large hockey-player husband. When Simone finally reached Morgan, she laid her hand on his arm. He briefly looked at it but not at her and offered not a word of greeting.

"You're angry with me," she said softly.

He almost looked at her then, but checked himself in time. Instead, he practically turned his back on her. "Don't be ridiculous. Why would I be angry with you?"

Seeing no point in playing that game, she told him forthrightly, "I thought Brooks was inviting both of us to dinner."

That shocked a glance out of him, but he quickly covered. "You're not that naive."

"I guess I am."

"Well, I'm sure you enjoyed yourself anyway."

"I did, actually. Brooks is an interesting man and a good friend."

Morgan seemed to lose his patience then, prodding his aunt rather loudly. "Aunt Odelia, would you mind?"

As he was already crowding past her, the poor old dear gasped a confused, "Oh!" and pressed against her husband, who frowned at Morgan as he charged past them up the aisle. Being smaller, Simone was able to slip by without making physical contact, offering an apologetic grimace as she did so. She almost had to run to catch up, zigzagging around people who had stopped to chat.

"Are we really going to argue about this?" she asked breathlessly, drawing near to him.

"Who's arguing? I'm not arguing," he tossed over his shoulder, plowing on toward the doors.

"Well, what are we doing, then?" She wanted to know.

He stopped dead in his tracks. She smacked right into him. He turned and caught her before she bounced into the end of the nearest pew.

"I don't know," he answered, looking her straight in the eye. "I simply do not know."

With that, he released her, turned and fled. She had no other word for it.

Frustrated and confused, Simone dithered, her hands going to her hair. God knew she'd messed up everything in her life, every relationship, every chance, every hope to this very point. But if He had a plan for her, for them, if she could get it right just once, then this had to be it. *Sweet Lord, please let this be it!* She stiffened her spine and marched off after him, up the aisle and into the grand foyer of the magnificent Spanish revival church.

Tiptoeing, she caught sight of Morgan as he slipped out the far right door. She hurried after him, knowing that if she didn't catch him on the front steps, she'd lose him. Shoving the heavy, carved door open, she pushed out into the autumn sunshine and immediately spied Morgan on the sidewalk, speaking to his cousin Phillip, her brother-in-law. Phillip spotted her and lifted a hand in greeting before jogging up the stairs to meet her as she quickly began to descend.

"We didn't think to get a phone number," he began, "and Chester said you'd be here, so I thought I'd swing by to try to catch you."

"Is there a problem?" she asked tensely, concentrating on negotiating the steps as rapidly as possible without falling.

"No, no, but because everyone around Chatam House usually fends for themselves on Sunday, we figured you might take off on your own before we could catch you there."

The Chatam sisters were well known for "eating simple" on the Lord's Day, to spare their staff the work of meal preparation and the resulting cleanup. Simone usually made a sandwich, skipped lunch entirely or headed over to the mission to pick up a snack there. None of that explained why Phillip was looking for her, however, so Morgan did.

"Phillip and Carissa would like you to have dinner with them at their house today."

That brought her up short. She was almost afraid to believe him. "Dinner?"

She looked to Phillip for confirmation. He smiled in invitation.

"You haven't met the children yet."

Tears rose in Simone's eyes. "I would love to do that, but…are you sure?"

Phillip lifted his very broad shoulders. "I'm not saying it won't be a little awkward. Okay, maybe a lot awkward. But you're sisters. You need to work this out."

She licked her lips, trying to maintain her composure, and admitted, "I really want to, but I'm a terrible coward."

"That's a bald-faced lie," Morgan refuted.

"No, I really am," she insisted. "Would you go with me?"

She thought for one horrible moment that he might refuse, but then he looked to Phillip, who shrugged.

"Family's family, dude. Come on over."

Morgan sighed and conceded. "I don't have anything better to do."

Simone held out her hand. Morgan shook his head, gave a self-deprecating snort and clasped her hand in his much stronger one. She burbled a laugh, dashing at tears with a knuckle.

"You'd better change out of your Sunday best," Phillip warned, heading off down the sidewalk.

"What should I wear?" Simone called after him anxiously.

"Something sturdy!" he shouted.

She looked at Morgan, but he just raised his eyebrows. "Jeans it is. Pick you up in twenty minutes?"

She nodded hopefully and hurried back into the church to tell the Chatams about her dinner plans. They were very accommodating and drove her straightaway back to the house, where she spent precious minutes dithering over what to wear. In the end, she chose the aforementioned jeans, her boots and a claret-red textured knit sweater with a boat-neck. Morgan and his aunties waited at the foot of the stairs when she came down, Kent having gone off to prepare the meal.

"There now," Hypatia said, coming forward to give Simone a quick hug, "I knew we could rely on your sister's sweet nature and good sense."

"Better hers than mine," Simone quipped, but the joke fell flat, too true to be funny.

"Let's go before you beat yourself to a pulp," Morgan interjected.

"Try to relax," Hypatia counseled.

"And give this to Grace from me," Odelia said, handing over a length of bright pink feathered boa. As if to legitimize the gift, she'd draped herself in three of the things, all in different colors, twining one in her hair.

"This is for Tucker," Magnolia announced, coming forward with a pinecone.

"And this is for Nathan," Hypatia said, pulling a small faded hardbound book from her pocket. "It's very old and should be handled with care. Be sure he sees the inscription."

On the trip across town, Simone cradling the gifts for the children, Morgan told her about Phillip and Carissa, how they'd met at a grief recovery session facilitated by Hub and fallen in love while both were living at Chatam House, where Phillip had moved after giving up mountain climbing when some friends and coworkers had died in an accident. Carissa and the children had been forced to accept Chatam House charity after the death of Carissa and Simone's father. Disabled by his disease, he'd been living in a subsidized apartment when Carissa and the children had moved in with him after the bank had foreclosed on their home. They couldn't stay once the disabled person entitled to the subsidy had departed. Together, Phillip and Carissa had started a surprisingly successful smart-app design business, which they ran from their home, which turned out to be in an older neighborhood just a couple blocks off Main Street.

The place had two driveways, one on each side of the white-brick-and-brown-stone house. Even with grass tanned by frost and the surrounding trees and crape myrtles bare, the evergreen shrubbery and climbing ivy added greenery to the landscape. Morgan had driven the sedan and parked in front of a spacious three-car garage, as the other driveway was for business use.

"I saw the offices from the inside when I was here for the wedding. They have a pool, by the way."

"That's nice."

They strolled up the meandering walkway, both anxious and reluctant.

"Nervous?" Morgan asked.

"Very. I feel sick to my stomach."

The front door, inlaid with leaded glass, had been painted a shade of red very like that of Simone's sweater. It opened suddenly and a small figure darted through it. Coming to rest right at Simone's toes, she turned her piquant face up and studied the pair of them. Her hair was longer and thicker than Simone's and perhaps half a shade lighter, and her nose was little more than a suggestion, but the resemblance was breathtaking.

"You must be Grace," Simone said, hoping the child couldn't hear the quiver in her voice.

"You're the runned-away one," she announced un-abashedly.

"Now I'm the came-back one," Simone said.

Grace giggled and pointed at the boa in Simone's hand. "That's for me, I figger."

"From Mrs. Monroe," Simone said, draping it around the girl's neck.

"Who?"

"Aunt Odelia," Morgan clarified.

"Oh! Auntie Od," the child crowed, turning toward the house and waving for them to follow.

Simone blinked at Morgan. "Surely no one calls her that."

"Not to her face," Morgan muttered.

Grace ran to the door, which remained open, stuck her head inside and bawled, "They're here!"

Immediately two boys appeared, their heads stacked one atop the other. The shorter, younger one looked very like his late father. The older, taller boy wore glasses and a very serious expression. Simone saw something of her own father in him.

The younger ran forward, hand outstretched, and demanded, "What did you bring me?"

Simone tossed Morgan a wry smile before producing the pinecone.

The boy whipped around and shouted, "Dad, I need a shovel!"

Phillip appeared in the open doorway, a wriggling baby in ruffled pink held against his chest. Again, Simone looked to Morgan, but he just shrugged, obviously as puzzled as she was by this tiny surprise.

"What for?" Phillip wanted to know.

"To plant a tree."

"That's not a tree," the older boy said.

"Is so."

"Is not."

"Is so! Aunt Mags explained—"

"They're *seeds*."

"Tree seeds, so it's the same thing."

"Is not."

"Is so. Dad, can I get a shovel?"

"Go ahead. Just don't plant any fingers or toes."

The boy loped off in the direction of the garage.

"You must be Nathan," Simone said to the older boy.

He nodded and said, "Tucker's rude."

Simone ignored that and held out the book, which

was small enough to fit comfortably in the palm of her hand. "Miss Hypatia sent this to you. She said to tell you that it's very old and for you to read the inscription inside."

The boy stepped down off the small covered stoop and took the book from her. Opening it carefully, he thumbed through the first few pages. He smiled up at Phillip then.

"This was Doc Doc's."

Phillip clapped the boy on the shoulder, nodding, before saying to Simone, "That's my father. His name is Murdock, Doc for short, and he's a doctor, so the kids call him Doc Doc."

"I'll tell Mom they're here," Nathan said, folding the book closed and disappearing back into the house.

"Dad and Nathan are very fond of each other," Phillip said to Morgan. "Who'd a thunk it, right?"

Morgan chuckled. "What I want to know is what that is attached to your chest."

Phillip jiggled the wriggling, cooing bundle in his arms. "You don't know a cousin when you see one? This is Marie Ella. We're babysitting Asher's little girl. I think my big brother's trying to give me ideas, like we don't have enough rug rats running around here."

"Asher is the attorney, yes?" Simone asked, trying not to stare covetously at the baby.

"Asher is the attorney, yes," Phillip said, backing out of the doorway and motioning for them to enter.

"He's helping a friend of mine," Simone said as they stepped up into a small entry that was really nothing more than a space set apart by a short wall.

"That's our Ash," Phillip noted, leading them into an enormous great room tiled with gleaming vanilla ceramic. A large living area furnished with a comfy sectional sofa and numerous chairs gave way to a lovely wrought-iron dining set that stood before a massive fireplace, behind which sprawled the kitchen. The whole of it was bookended by window seats in the living area and an entire wall of glass in the kitchen, overlooking a gorgeous pool and backyard.

"It's stunning," Simone said.

"We like it," Phillip told her proudly.

He covered Marie Ella's ear with an enormous hand and pressed her little head to his chest. She didn't like it much, but he didn't burst her eardrums when he shouted, "Honey!"

Carissa came out of a hallway on the left, straightening the hem of a top she had obviously just pulled over her head. "I'm coming. I'm coming."

"I think she's tried on every blouse she owns today," Phillip divulged.

"I have not!" Carissa snapped. "Only maybe half of them."

"You look beautiful," Simone said sincerely.

"She's a knockout," Phillip bragged.

"Oh, you." She reached up and plucked the baby out of his arms, but as she did so, she turned her face up, and he kissed her soundly, lingering at it as long as she would let him.

Grace suddenly pirouetted through the room, giggling. "They kiss all the time!"

"Hush up," Nathan ordered, popping up from the couch, his nose stuck in the book.

"Only if you'll play ballerina with me."

"Okay, come around here and dance for me. I'll be your audience."

As Grace began to sing and dance her way around the sectional sofa, Carissa happened to glance through the front window.

"Phillip!" she exclaimed. "What is that child doing?"

"Tucker? Oh, he's just digging a hole to plant a tree."

"It's not a tree," Nathan argued. "It's a pinecone."

"He'll ruin the grass," Carissa complained over Grace's singing.

"I'm going to resod in the spring anyway," was Phillip's laconic reply.

Grace hit a high note, twirled and bowed. "Now the song's about rainbows," she announced, launching into another aria.

Carissa rolled her eyes, shifted the baby onto her

hip and waved at Simone, saying, "Let's go into the kitchen. Phillip, try to corral the kids, will you?"

"Sure, honey."

Simone glanced at Morgan, who looked a bit shell-shocked, and followed her sister. Carissa pointed to a tall stool at a gleaming granite counter. "Sit there." She then promptly handed over the baby.

Just like that, Simone found herself ensconced in her sister's kitchen with the sweet little bundle in her lap and a lump in her throat. She was an adorable baby, all soft and pudgy, with dark curly hair and big dark eyes. Cooing and laughing, she waved her arms and kicked her tiny feet, perfectly content.

"Hello," Simone said, wondering if this was how it was to be, trying not to fall in love with every baby she met for the rest of her life. "How old is she?"

"About six months," Carissa said, checking something in the oven. "I hope you're hungry. You're too thin, you know."

"Yes, I know."

"The cancer?"

"Partly," Simone answered. "Partly depression, I think." How surprisingly easy it was to confide in her sister. After all this time, even with all the resentments and distance, she was still just Carissa.

"Over Dad?"

"That's some of it."

"Your marriage?"

"Not really. We weren't together very long before the cancer hit."

Carissa reached into the stainless steel refrigerator for a salad. "That's what ended it?"

Simone nodded. "Serious illness does strange things to people, makes them or breaks them. It broke us apart, and in some ways it broke me. In other ways, it made me."

"That makes a kind of sense," Carissa said. "More than you not letting us know you were here."

"Carissa," Simone began, but her sister lifted a hand.

"I don't want to talk about that. Whatever crazy notions you have in your head about that, you can just get over them. But you're going to have to let Mom know, Lyla."

Simone winced at the old name, but she wouldn't state a preference, and she wouldn't argue about letting Alexandra know she was in town, though she'd been hoping for a few more days' reprieve, at least.

"Whatever you think best."

"I'll set something up for one evening this week, then," Carissa told her.

Simone nodded glumly.

"She's probably going to want to come here," Carissa said, grimacing, "though I'd rather she didn't. That's awful, I know, but you remember how she is. She comes in and picks apart everything in the place.

I always want to move and forget to leave a forwarding address after she's been here."

"Hasn't changed much, then, I take it," Simone murmured.

"She has, actually," Carissa said, narrowing her eyes accusingly. "She's gotten worse, and I expect you to bear the brunt from now on."

"I suppose I deserve that," Simone muttered.

"You certainly do. Still, a neutral meeting place would be best the first time out," Carissa mused, "and I doubt we could get her back to Chatam House even if the aunties would be kind enough to agree. They didn't exactly hit it off."

"What about the mission where I work part-time?" Simone wondered. "I think Pastor Hub might agree."

Carissa brightened. "Uncle Hubner is a sweetie. I'm sure we can work something out with him."

Just then, Marie Ella let loose with a loud, foul-smelling grunt.

Carissa and Simone in unison cried, "Ew!"

"She is no lady when it comes to filling her diapers," Carissa exclaimed, waving a hand in front of her face. "Get her out of the kitchen, would you?"

Simone hopped down off the stool and carried the now grimacing baby draped over one arm into the living area. The men, who were seated at the dining table, both jumped up and fled as she approached.

"Yow! What is that?" Morgan demanded.

"That's Marie Ella," Phillip said. "She's a stinker. A sweetheart, but a stinker."

Not knowing what else to do, Simone carried the baby toward him. Surely he had dealt with this before.

"Oh, no," he said, jumping out of the way. "Everything you need is right down that hall." He pointed, adding, "Last door at the end."

"But—"

He craned his head, looking toward the front windows. "That kid's digging a hole big enough to bury himself. I better go supervise." Nathan and Grace, both holding their noses, were already out the door.

"I'll help," Morgan volunteered, following quickly after him.

"Morgan!"

He hesitated long enough to shake his head. "I'm the old bachelor here. Remember?"

Before he pulled the door closed, Phillip had the temerity to wink at her and chortle, "Welcome home, Lyla Simone."

"Oh!" She heaved a great sigh and held Marie Ella out at arm's length, muttering, "Where's a clothespin when you need one?"

Suddenly the little one screwed up her face and howled, no happier with her situation than anyone else apparently.

Ten minutes later, having found the right room and all the necessary accoutrements, including disposable plastic gloves—Marie Ella obviously having been a frequent visitor—the offending mass and odor had been disposed of, and a clean, happy baby had once again charmed Simone with her winsome, toothless smile. Carissa came in.

"Dinner's ready. I have Phillip and Morgan setting the table."

"Serves them right, abandoning me on the field of battle."

Carissa grinned. "Well, you know how it is. Phillip is great with the kids, but even he has his limits, and I don't imagine Morgan has had much experience."

"Neither have I," Simone complained, and then, quite without meaning to, she blurted, "and I probably never will."

"Sure you will," Carissa said dismissively. "You always think it'll never happen to you, but you'll be having babies before you know it."

Simone burst into tears before she even knew it was going to happen.

"Lyla!" Carissa dropped down next to her. "What's this?"

Simone gasped out what the cancer had taken from her, desperately needing to say it when before she hadn't wanted to talk about it at all except with Morgan. She'd only told Rina to try to help her see what a gift her baby was.

"Oh, honey," Carissa crooned, gathering her close. "I'm so sorry, so very sorry."

It was such a comfort, more comfort than any other words or any other hug. "Thank you."

"I had no idea."

"I know. I know. I didn't mean to spill it like that, but suddenly I just had to tell you."

"Of course you did. But it's not the end of the world. You can always adopt."

"I don't know. Maybe. There can be so many problems with that. I just don't know."

"Hey," Carissa told her, "you never know what God's got in the works. Look at me. Virtually unmarriageable one day and the next…"

Simone snorted, but Carissa insisted.

"No, really. Who wants a poor-as-a-church-mouse widow with three kids? Next thing I know, that hunk out there has roped me into developing reality apps and LOVE in capital letters. He's the most laid-back man on the face of the earth, too, and he has to be, to put up with my three terrors. It's a crisis an hour around here, and he thrives on it. God made him just for me, Lyla. I believe it heart and soul. He's got a plan for you, too."

They sat together, holding each other close, until Simone looked up and saw Phillip standing quietly in the doorway, a patient smile on his ruggedly handsome face. Simone realized suddenly that the children were screaming at the tops of their lungs and poor Morgan was probably pulling his hair out.

She sat up straight, dried her eyes and declared, "I'm starving."

Carissa gave a watery chuckle and plucked Marie Ella off the bed. Turning and rising in one swift motion, she thrust the baby into Phillip's hands, proving that she'd known he was there all along.

"Here, macho man. Take care of this."

As Carissa slipped around him, he winked at Simone and tipped the baby over his shoulder. She erupted in giggles.

It was a delightful sound. Simone felt lighter than she had in days. Not even the upcoming meeting with her mother could cloud this moment.

She had lost much, cost herself much, but she had a sister again and faith that God had a plan for her.

She could only hope and pray that the plan included Morgan.

Chapter Thirteen

"I wasn't this tired after the amusement park," Morgan admitted, walking Simone up onto the porch of Chatam House about a quarter of four on Sunday afternoon. "I don't know how Phillip does it. He actually seems to thrive on the chaos."

"I think he's the biggest kid in the family," Simone said.

"Maybe that's why he's so good with them," Morgan mused. "Did you see the way he handled the baby? I'd never have pegged Phillip for a nursemaid."

"She's a very sweet, easy baby," Simone pointed out dreamily.

"Especially considering that she's half skunk," Morgan muttered.

Simone spluttered with laughter. "She is rather pungent at times."

"*Every* time, according to Phillip. Apparently she's become a family legend."

"Poor darling," Simone giggled. "What awful stories they're going to embarrass her with when she's older."

"The tale is bound to be lost in the heaps of Chatam progeny to come," Morgan said thoughtlessly. "Kaylie's already expecting, and I hear my baby brother, Chandler, is feeling some pressure to add to his herd. Then there's Petra and Dale, Phillip's older sister and her husband. Also, I'm told that my Leland cousin Reeves and his wife have been trying for some time."

Simone looked positively stricken. He wanted to cut out his tongue. After an awkward moment, she changed the subject with an endearing determination. "You're kin to Brooks?"

Morgan's mood went from wretched to brutal in a snap. He worked hard to keep the snarl out of his voice. "Brooks didn't tell you?"

"No."

"We're only related by marriage, if that. His uncle Thomas was married to my aunt Dorinda, the youngest sister of Hub, Hypatia, Magnolia, Odelia and Murdock, in that order. Anyway, Dorinda and Thomas divorced years and years ago. She remarried and moved to California. Thomas and wife number three, I think, are still around. It's really more that Brooks and I have common relatives. My cousin Reeves is also his cousin. That's all there is to it." Morgan told himself to be glad that she'd reminded him why he should be keeping his distance from her. It was too easy to forget.

"I see." To his chagrin, she walked over to one of the wrought-iron chairs beside the front door and sat down, saying, "You never asked me about my dinner with Brooks."

"No, and I don't intend to," he stated firmly.

"That's too bad," she said, "because I'm going to tell you about it anyway." She patted the chair next to her.

"Look, Simone," he began, but she fixed him with a steely stare and ordered him to sit down. Feeling it would be churlish, if not downright cowardly, to do anything else, he sat, sliding well back in the chair and crossing his legs.

"First of all," she said, "I'm not the least bit interested in Brooks Leland."

Morgan tried not to let loose a smile at that. The thing squirmed around on his lips for a while before he got a firm hold on it, but he managed. Saying what he needed to say was more difficult, but he managed that, too.

"You should be. Brooks is a fine man. And a doctor." *Duh.* "He's…closer to your age."

"Oh, please."

"He is. A few years."

"Yes, yes, you're quite right," she agreed. "He's also intelligent and caring and handsome."

Well, that was more than Morgan wanted to hear.

"Yeah, he's a paragon. The point is—"

"The point is I'm already interested in someone else. More than interested, really."

Morgan's heart thunked hopefully. Him. She had to mean him. Didn't she?

No, of course she didn't. Men were probably lined up around the block just waiting for a chance at this woman—younger men, without restrictions and emotional baggage the size of V-8 engines.

"That's great," he said, trying to sound as though he meant it. He clapped his hands to the narrow arms of the metal chair and prepared to rise. "I'm happy for you."

"You should be," she said, putting a hand in the center of his chest and pushing him back down. "You really are the dumbest smart man alive, aren't you?"

He glowered as the full meaning of what she'd said settled in. "That's one of Brooks's pet sayings. You two were discussing me, weren't you?"

"Don't change the subject," she snapped. "When I'm shamelessly throwing myself at you, the least you can do is make a halfhearted attempt to catch me."

Stunned, he bleated, *"Whaat?"*

"You heard me," she retorted petulantly.

And that's when she kissed him. Again.

And that's when he kissed her back. Again.

But honestly, what was a man supposed to do when a woman, *the* woman he hadn't been able to get out of his head for more than ten seconds running in weeks, was right there, pressing her sweet lips against his, smelling like a garden and tasting like ambrosia—not that too-salty chicken casserole they'd had for Sunday dinner—and twining her arms about his neck? How could he not palm the back of her head and slide his arm about her shoulders to draw her close? What was so wrong about just floating for a minute or two—or five—in the misty cloud of elation that her kiss brought him?

He wondered how long it had been since he'd really wanted anything, anyone, and he wasn't sure now that he ever really had before this, and that was a startling discovery at his age. When at last he found the strength to pull back, she had the dreamy look that every man wanted to believe he could put on a woman's face. Until reality slapped him right upside his ego.

"Aw, I can't keep doing this!" he told himself as much as her.

She huffed out a sigh of pure disgust. "I would like to know why not."

"Simone, I am not the man for you," he stated flatly.

"I think you are."

"I'm too old."

"Ha!" She laughed, one hand coming up to press against her lips. "I think not."

He did not need reminding of that kiss. Shooting up to his feet, he began to pace.

"Then put it another way. You're too young."

She tucked her chin and rolled those big, beautiful eyes up at him. "Surely you can do better than that. I've been on my own since I was sixteen. I'll tell you something else. I tried a relationship with a man my own age. It is not an experience I care to repeat, and I think he should wait at least ten or fifteen years before he tries it again, too. Do you honestly think I'm not mature enough to know my own mind?"

Morgan didn't dare concede the point, but in truth she was the most mature twenty-six-year-old he'd ever met, and he'd met *many,* so he simply tried another tactic.

"Simone, you're a *student,* and for me that's poison."

She tucked one dainty boot beneath her, tilted her head and said, "Once I'm on staff at the college, that won't matter."

That rocked him. So she had tumbled to that loophole in the college policy, had she? He didn't think his father had let that particular cat out, but who else might have opened the bag? The answer was all too plain.

"Brooks told you, did he?"

She inclined her head in an elegant nod. "He did. He told me more besides."

Morgan folded his arms. "Such as?"

She straightened, pressed her hands together

primly, looked him right in the face and nearly felled him with, "Brigitte knew about the brain tumor before she broke your engagement."

He staggered and dropped down onto the chair again. "What is that you're saying?"

"She knew about the brain tumor before she broke your engagement."

He couldn't speak, his mind whirling, for several seconds. "But…"

"Brooks married her even though he knew she was dying."

The implications were enormous, but one thing stood out. "Why didn't they tell me?"

"They wanted to spare you as much as they could," Simone told him sympathetically. "Brooks said he knew as soon as she broke her engagement to you that God's plan was for him and her, not you and her. But he loved her, Morgan. He loved her so much, and the time they had together was worth the world to him."

Still reeling, Morgan mumbled, "He told you all this, but not me?"

"Yes," Simone said, "because he wants us not to be afraid of the possibility of my cancer returning. But it isn't the same. I see that even if he doesn't. Her fate was sealed. Anyone who gets involved with me is taking an unknown risk," she went on. "I know it's asking a lot, Morgan, and I don't blame you at all, if that's why—"

"You think that's the reason I keep trying to do what I know I should with you?" he interrupted, appalled.

"Why you're trying to push me away, you mean."

"That's not it! Give me some credit, will you? I have some faith, you know."

"Then what?"

"Sweetheart," he said urgently, "don't you understand that with a younger man you could easily adopt children but with me it's not likely?"

"And you're young enough to still father children of your own," she countered wistfully, "but you'd never have that chance with me."

Astounded, he shook his head. "Simone, it's been so long since I thought about having children that I don't even know how I feel about that now." He rubbed a hand over his face, muttering, "Especially after today."

"Not all households are like my sister's," she told him wryly.

"That's a relief," he said, shaking his head at the thought of Grace standing in her chair and performing a four-year-old's version of "Yankee Doodle *Daddy*" while her mother scolded and Phillip applauded.

"I couldn't live in that kind of chaos, either," Simone said, "but I have to admit that I would grab at any opportunity to have a child."

"I know," Morgan said, "and I'm not sure that time hasn't passed me by entirely."

"So where does that leave us?" she asked.

"That I don't know," he admitted, gusting a sigh.

She bit her lip, that beautiful, luscious lower lip. He almost groaned.

"Don't throw me over yet," she pleaded. "Let's just give it some time to see what God has planned."

"At this point, I can't see anything else to do," Morgan conceded, cupping her sweet face with his hand. "I'm an abject failure at getting rid of you. Funny, I've never failed at that before. I'm a master at it."

"Even the professor has to learn a lesson from time to time," she teased.

He drew his brows together. "I've learned a few things today."

"I guess we both have," she said, and he suddenly realized how tired she looked.

"You look beat. Go in and get some rest."

Nodding, she got to her feet. "It's more emotional than physical, but it's a good tired this time. You were right about Carissa. We had a long talk. She told me about Dad and her husband Tom."

"I'm glad."

"I expect we have our moments ahead of us, but for now I have my sister back."

"Answered prayer there," he said, turning her toward the door.

"Truly. Thank you for being with me today. I owe you for this one."

He chuckled. "You do. You really do."

She slid him a look over her shoulder then, saying, "But that doesn't mean you don't have to come with me to meet my mother. And after that if you don't go running for the hills, then you're a better man than even I think you are, Professor Chatam, and that's saying a lot."

He was grinning like the fool that he undoubtedly was when the door closed behind her, for they were no closer, really, to solving anything. The years hadn't diminished. She was still a student and forbidden territory that he just kept crossing. Someday soon, he was going to get caught at it. And that baby thing just kept getting bigger and bigger. But he wasn't sure now that he really even had a choice when it came to Lyla Simone Worth Guilland. He was helplessly, hopelessly in her thrall, and God was going to have to get him out of this one.

The meeting with Simone's mother, Alexandra Hedgespeth, and her husband, Leander, was set for the following Saturday afternoon at the mission. Hub volunteered to be there. Morgan was shocked to find that Chester and Hilda wanted no part of the meeting. That, as much if not more than Simone's comments, should have prepared him for what he would find when he escorted Simone into his father's crowded office, but though he'd caught a glimpse of Alexandra at Phillip and Carissa's wedding, she hadn't bothered to stop by the reception, so he had no real idea that the attractive blonde was all plastic veneer outside and venom inside.

Simone had dressed with care in a chic moss-green knit sheath with a straight-across-the-shoulders neckline that called attention to her long, graceful neck and regal carriage. The narrow sleeves belled at the wrists, showing off her delicate, feminine hands, and the midcalf length of the narrow skirt worked well with her boots. She'd added a soft suede belt with fringed ends and tied it loosely, letting it drape about her hips. He thought she looked smashing, and he'd have been proud to walk into any faculty function with her on his arm. Yet she'd barely entered the room before her mother attacked.

"What have you done to yourself? You're skinny as a rail! You're a drug addict, aren't you?" Seated in front of his desk, Alexandra looked to Hub for confirmation, saying, "That's what happens to kids who run away from home, isn't it? You must see it all the time."

"Rarely, actually," Hub replied, rocking back in his chair.

"I'm not a drug addict, Mother," Simone said calmly, sinking down into the empty chair at Alexandra's side. Carissa was seated on a small couch tucked up against the wall. Phillip folded himself down next to her after Simone sat. Morgan went to lean against the end of his father's desk nearest Simone. "And hello, it's nice to see you," Simone went on. "How have you been?"

"Don't give me that," Alexandra snapped, tossing her long poufy blond hair. Up close, Morgan could tell that she'd had plastic surgery and wore impossibly long fake nails, as well as a ton of cosmetics. "Your sister tells me that you've been in town for months without letting anyone know."

"Can't imagine why," Simone muttered.

"And you never used to be this skinny," Alexandra went on. "If anything, you were a bit on the chunky side."

"I was a bit on the chunky side at fifteen," Phillip announced proudly, making Morgan chuckle.

"You were, weren't you? Then you suddenly shot up six inches and got thin."

Simone sent Phillip a grateful glance. At the same time, Simone's stepfather shifted away from the corner by the door where he stood and affably stated, "I was always on the chunky side myself. Have to work out continuously to stay in shape." He patted his firm middle with an overly tanned hand, but upon receiving a venomous glare from his wife, Leander immediately subsided back into his corner.

"I want to know what is going on with you, Lyla Simone, and I want to know it now."

"If you must know," Simone divulged softly, "I've been ill."

Alexandra's next question had everyone in the room gasping. "Was it sexually transmitted?"

Simone's face bloomed bloodred, and Morgan immediately reached for her hand, exclaiming, "Of course not!"

At the same time, Carissa said, "No!"

Simone gathered her dignity and informed her mother, "I had cancer."

Realizing that she'd embarrassed herself, Alexandra dug in her voluminous handbag and came up with a tissue, with which she carefully dabbed her eyes and nose, though the hanky remained suspiciously dry.

"Oh, my poor child. Just like your father."

Over the next ten minutes, Alexandra dragged one disconcerting fact after another out of Simone, and nothing anyone else said could prevent it. What Simone refused to say, Alexandra deduced until she and everyone else in the room had the whole ugly picture laid bare before them.

"And now you've returned to us," Alexandra gushed, working her dry hanky, "battered and broken, half a woman."

Morgan had borne all he could stand. He came up off the corner of the desk and pulled Simone to her feet, wrapping his arms around her. "That is enough! How dare you say such things?"

Alexandra leaped up, her stiletto heels clicking on the concrete floor. "And what business is it of yours? I'm not at all clear on who you are and what you're doing here."

He wasn't clear on that himself, but he wasn't about to tell her.

"This is my son Morgan," Hubner said with a wave of his hand. "I'm afraid we didn't make proper introductions earlier."

"Morgan's my friend," Simone said huskily, and he knew immediately that she was trying to protect him, that she didn't want her mother to know that he was a professor at the Bible college or her faculty adviser. If he'd had the sense God gave bean sprouts, he'd let go of her, but somehow he couldn't do it. Instead he glared at Alexandra Hedgespeth, who melted before his very eyes.

"Another Chatam," she purred. "Well, I did *something* right with you girls."

Carissa dropped her head into her hands, groaning. At the same time, Simone rolled her eyes and looked away, practically turning her face into Morgan's chest. Hub, God bless him, rocked forward in his chair, pushed back from his desk and calmly climbed to his feet, putting an end to the fiasco.

"Well, I thank you all for coming. Mr. and Mrs. Hedgespeth, Phillip will see you out."

"My pleasure," Phillip said, bouncing up to his full height in a single exuberant motion.

Alexandra lifted her chin mutinously, and in that one gesture, Morgan saw a bit of Simone in her, but just in that one tiny mannerism, which he would happily tell Simone as soon as he got her alone. Fortunately for everyone involved, Leander Hedgespeth showed some backbone and came forward to grasp his wife by the arm and tug her toward the door. She jerked as if he'd stabbed her, but after only a moment's silent communication between the two, she softened her stance and finally did something halfway motherly. She came forward to pretend to hug Simone and kiss the air next to her cheek. Simone pulled far enough away from Morgan to accept this phony show of affection.

"I trust I'll see you again soon," Alexandra said.

"Goodbye, Mother" was Simone's noncommittal answer.

Alexandra then turned to Carissa, trilling her a little wave. "Give the children my best."

"Of course," Carissa told her drily.

As soon as the door closed at her back, Simone addressed her sister. "Please tell me you didn't give her my cell phone number."

Carissa shook her head. "She doesn't even have *my* cell phone number."

Simone closed her eyes in gratitude. "Thank you."

Carissa chuckled. "Don't mention it. I figure if I give her your number, you'll give her mine."

"In a heartbeat," Simone threatened drolly, and

they shared a smile. Then Simone shook her head. "Poor Mother. How many does this make?"

"Marriages?" Carissa asked. "Not sure. She's off the radar for long stretches. This one's not such a bad guy, but he's a lot younger than he looks, and I fear it's not going to last. I understand he wants to be a father."

Simone's face fell. She stared at the door wistfully. "Poor man. And poor Mother. She has no idea how to be happy."

"We've invited her to church," Carissa said, rising to wander closer to her sister, "but she thinks I've nose-dived right off the deep end into religious zealotry."

"Maybe the two of us together can make some inroads," Simone suggested, a pleased smile on her face.

"We'll certainly be praying along those lines," Hub interjected.

"Thank you," Carissa told him. "Now I'd better go rescue my husband. If I know Alexandra, and I do, she's holding him hostage with a litany of complaints starting in my infancy." She looked at Morgan then, adding, "And he's every bit as protective as the professor." She grinned at Simone, saying, "You've just got to like these Chatam men, don't you?" With that she swept from the room.

"*Like* is a mild word for what I feel," Simone said softly, turning to face Morgan. Her eyes were huge and warm and brimming with an emotion that took his breath away. It was all he could do not to pull her to him then and there and declare that he'd move mountains to make her his. Fortunately, his father saved him.

"Simone," he said, "before you go, I ought to tell you that Asher asked me to speak with your friend Rina yesterday."

She immediately switched her attention to Hubner. "Oh?"

"She seems quite settled on the decision to give up her child for adoption. I thought you'd want to know."

Simone bit her lip, and Morgan could see that she was struggling for composure. How difficult it must have been for her to know that another young woman could give up a child when she would give anything for the chance to have one. Finally, she spoke.

"Perhaps it's best."

"We can but hope and trust God in the matter," Hub said, and Simone nodded.

Searching for a way to change the subject and lighten the mood, Morgan turned Simone for the door, saying, "Come on. I'm taking you to dinner. In case you didn't know, you're apparently too thin."

She chuckled as he led her away from his father's desk. "So I hear."

"Actually," he told her, "I think you look spectacular and that your mother would kill to be able to wear that dress."

Simone laughed outright at that. He walked her through the door then looked back at his dad, who smiled and saluted in approval. Morgan made a fist and tapped it over his heart. The last glimpse he had of his dad before he pulled the door closed was of Hubner sitting down again and folding his hands in prayer.

After that Saturday, Simone could not have been more in love with Morgan Chatam if he'd come complete with white charger and a suit of armor.

"Do not ever again," he told her at dinner in the same little French bistro where they'd dined alone the first time, "let me hear you say anything remotely equating yourself with your mother."

"But, Morgan," she argued, "running away was selfish and cruel to the people who loved me, my father, especially. It was exactly the sort of thing my mother did to him. I've accepted and confessed that."

"And there's the difference," he pointed out. "That was then. This is now. You've accepted responsibility for past mistakes and you've accomplished laudable things all on your own. Plus, you're helping others. Besides, your beauty is completely genuine. I don't blame anyone for wanting to look their best, but some people take it too far. It becomes an obsession with them. What's more, I suspect she knows that you don't even have to try to be beautiful."

Simone couldn't help blushing over such a pretty

compliment as that. Neither could she help thinking that Brooks was right about Morgan's feelings for her and that God must intend for the two of them to be together. It all just made a wonderful, glorious sense, which was why Monday's news came as such a crushing blow.

She didn't get the job.

The shattering announcement came as a form letter to her student mailbox.

"Thank you for applying," she read, "blah, blah, blah…a more qualified candidate, blah, blah, blah…"

Simone couldn't believe it. She'd been so sure that she'd discerned God's will for her and Morgan. When she handed the letter to Morgan after class that morning, he'd first joked about it.

"What's this? Is your mother demanding redress for your years of absence?"

"It isn't funny," Simone choked out, waiting for him to read the thing.

He'd grown somber after the first sentence. Finally, he wadded up the paper and slammed it into the trash can beside his desk. "Stupid of me not to see that coming."

"I guess I should've applied for more than the one position," she ventured woodenly.

He rubbed a hand over his face. "There haven't been any more openings."

That hit her like a sledgehammer. "Oh."

"Doesn't mean there won't be," he said, looking

up, but she could tell he was as disturbed by this turn of events as she was.

"Of course," she said, but he didn't believe it, and neither did she.

He'd been right all along. They weren't meant to be together. Sometimes a person just had to face facts.

"I guess I'd better go," she said, disappointed but unsurprised when he didn't try to stop her.

She felt as if she were wading through chest-deep water as she walked away and left him sitting there on the end of his desk, slumped and frowning. At least he seemed as dejected as she felt, but that didn't change anything.

No, it only made the disappointment that much harder to bear.

Chapter Fourteen

"My dear, I don't know what is bothering you, but I think it would do you good to go to prayer meeting," Hypatia said after knocking on Simone's bedroom door Wednesday evening. "Besides, Rina says that she will go if you do."

Simone smiled wanly and put on as brave a face as she could muster. She had floated in a miasma of disbelief these past two days. "What makes you think something is wrong with me?"

"You've retreated behind your bedroom door again, for one thing," Hypatia answered. "For another, you look like you've lost your best friend."

That was so apt that Simone had to work hard at not bursting into tears. "You know how it is when you talk yourself into believing something silly and then realize that you were dreaming all along."

"All I know," Hypatia told her kindly, "is that it can't hurt to go among your fellow Christians and join them in some earnest prayer. It might even take your mind off things."

That, Simone admitted privately, would be most welcome, and bringing Rina along couldn't hurt, either. She had tried to talk to the girl about keeping her baby, but Rina had insisted that she and the lawyer had everything under control. Simone really didn't know what was best in Rina's situation, anyway, and she couldn't be unbiased about it. They would both benefit from prayer.

"I'll get changed," Simone said. "Then I'll walk over to the carriage house and get Rina."

Hypatia patted her hand. "Very good."

Simone wasted no time trading her slouchy sweats for leggings, a wool skirt, a roomy cable-knit sweater and flats. A long wool scarf looped about her throat was enough to ward off even a mid-November chill in Texas. So armed, she went out to fetch Rina from the carriage house.

The girl had grown immensely in the two weeks since she'd come to Chatam House. Her belly literally filled out the maternity top that she wore with stretch pants, leaving no doubt as to her condition. Simone realized that Rina could not even see her feet as she negotiated the stairs. She was in a much better frame of mind, however, which is why Simone was so puzzled by her decision to give up her child.

"The misses say I can take a class for the college entrance exam," she reported excitedly, "and that there are grants and loans available, but I don't know. Do you really think I can do it? I wasn't a very good student before."

"There's nothing wrong with your brain, Rina," Simone told her. "You can do anything you set your mind to."

"Miss Hypatia says I should pray about it, but I feel so funny doing that. Does it work?"

Simone licked her lips. "It does, yes, when you're seeking God's will and not just your own."

"I'm not sure I understand that."

"Perhaps you'll find some answers tonight," Simone told her, thinking that she was the last person to be giving advice on seeking God's will rather than her own. It was seeking her own desires that had led her to believe that she and Morgan were meant to be together.

They walked back to the main house and got into the town car with Hypatia, Magnolia, Odelia and Kent, who drove their party to the church on the downtown square. The venerable old church sprawled over an entire city block, but it was the chapel in the back of the campus, rather than the soaring Spanish-style sanctuary, where Kent let them out. The two worship centers stood back-to-back. Though of significantly later construction, the chapel had much more of a Spanish-mission flavor to it, complete with adobe walls and archways. Built in the shape of a cross, it allowed groups to gather in four distinct areas around a central altar.

The instant she passed through the narthex, Simone's gaze found Morgan. He stood with his father near the center of the chapel, speaking quietly, his hands in the pockets of his khakis. As if drawn by a lodestone, his gaze met hers, and he started forward, but she quickly turned away, directing Rina to follow along behind Hypatia. She just didn't think she could calmly converse with him as if their world had not blown apart. For that very reason, she'd skipped his class that day. She had to have some distance to get a hold of her emotions. If he came to her now, she feared what he would say, and she would undoubtedly weep, and the whole situation would become a public spectacle, which was the last thing he needed. Apparently, he realized the wisdom of that, too, for when she took a seat in a row of chairs behind Hypatia and her sisters, she chanced a glance in his direction and saw that he was sitting, with his head bowed, between his father and his sister.

The meeting began with some singing. Simone did her best to participate, but her throat kept closing up. At one point, Rina leaned over and whispered, "Are you and the prof on the outs?"

Simone smiled and shook her head. "No, nothing like that."

"Oh, okay. You just seem so sad, and I can't help wondering why you're not together. Seems like you two ought to be together. You love him, don't you? He's sure got it for you."

"Rina, please don't speak of that here," Simone whispered urgently, hoping they couldn't be heard over the music.

"Why not? You're not ashamed, are you?"

"Of course not. We have nothing to be ashamed of. But it's…complicated."

"Is it 'cause you can't have kids?"

Simone glanced around them self-consciously. "Rina, please! Not now."

"Sorry," the girl muttered. "I just want to help."

"I know," Simone told her, sliding an arm around the girl's shoulders. "I appreciate that. I do." She mustered up a smile and tried to hide the heaviness of her heart.

Thankfully, the music ended and along with it, the opportunity for any sort of conversation. They took their seats, and the pastor read from the Bible before calling their attention to the printed list they'd received on the way inside. They prayed corporately for those on the list, all ill, grieving or in need of some sort of assistance. Then, section by section, the alcoves were closed off with curtains and the resulting four smaller groups were led by a facilitator in requesting individual prayer.

When it came Rina's turn to speak, she said, "I want this little girl to come out healthy and get a good life."

"It's a girl?" Simone exclaimed, clasping Rina's hand. "I didn't know."

"Just found out today," Rina told her.

"That's lovely." She realized then that everyone was looking at her. Did she have a prayer request? Tears filled her eyes, but she couldn't say it. She dared not, for Morgan's sake. Besides, how could she ask for the stars when God had already given her the moon? He'd spared her life, reunited her with her family, brought her to the Chatams, seen to it that she got a good education.... How could she be so ungrateful as to ask for more? Mutely, she shook her head, and the facilitator moved on.

After thirty or forty minutes, prayers came to an end, the curtains were drawn back, a final song was sung and they were dismissed with a blessing. Simone was glad she'd come. She felt a little more at peace, a little more centered—until she looked up and found Brooks looming over her.

"What is going on?" he asked in a no-nonsense voice.

Simone blinked at him, slowly rising to her feet. She could feel Rina hanging on every word that passed between them. "I'm not sure what you mean."

"Don't give me that. Morgan looks like someone shot his dog, and you don't look any happier."

Furrowing her brow, Simone tried to think of a politic way out of this, something that wouldn't embarrass Morgan. Finally, she stated the simple truth.

"I didn't get the job."

Brooks lifted both brows and blew out a disappointed sigh. "And you've taken that as some great sign, I suppose."

"How am I supposed to take it?"

"I don't know. Did you even pray about it?"

She tossed a gaze around the room. "Of course not."

"I mean in private."

She didn't know how to answer that, how to explain herself without everyone within earshot figuring out what they were talking about, and she imagined that everyone was listening in. Rina and Hypatia certainly were, and neither made any bones about it.

Brooks threw up his hands. "Simone, sometimes you just have to ask for what you want. Prayer isn't about motivating God to act or informing Him of your needs, but sometimes He just wants you to sit down, think it through and *ask* for what you want."

"That's right, dear," Hypatia volunteered. "There's no harm in asking for what you want. If it's not good for you, God can and will say no, but at least you'll have opened a dialogue on the matter, and eventually, if you're willing to invest the time and listen, you'll come to understand His mind concerning it."

She'd never thought of it that way. "I see." She tilted her head. "I guess, in a way, I've just been expecting Him to read my mind."

Hypatia chuckled. "He can certainly do that, but what you've been trying to do is read *His* mind."

Now Simone had to smile. "How right you are."

Just watching Brooks stand and talk to Simone was almost more than Morgan could bear. He'd been tormented by thoughts of them together before, but now just the idea that Brooks could publicly carry on a conversation with her without anyone thinking twice about it made Morgan want to smack things. Perhaps it was ridiculous—they'd been out to dinner together, after all—yet, somehow, after she'd been turned down for the job at BCBC, Morgan no longer felt comfortable approaching her in public, and he wouldn't go to her in private. That reeked too much of sneaking around.

He didn't know what to do, and it was eating him alive. He hadn't felt this torn up about Brigitte. If he was honest about it, once she and Brooks had gotten together, even Morgan had known it was right, though he'd been too stupid to admit it. After she'd died, grieving with Brooks had felt entirely appropriate, and Morgan hadn't had any problem taking a backseat then. Brooks had been devastated and a tower of strength at the same time. He'd warranted every show of support that had come his way, and Morgan had begrudged him none of it, but he resented every word that the man said to Simone standing in the church that evening. Something had to be done about this situation, and it was up to him to do it.

He'd prayed and prayed about this thing between him and Simone, and now he made a decision. Looking to his dad, he announced it.

"I'm going to make an appointment with the provost tomorrow."

Hub glanced in Simone's direction and asked, "Don't you think you should discuss it with her?"

"No. She'll try to talk me out of it, and I might be stupid enough to let her."

"You should pray about it together, Morgan," Hub advised.

"You're absolutely right," Morgan agreed, determination filling him.

He was tired of hiding behind well-meaning regulations and edicts, practically skulking around when he'd done nothing of which he should be ashamed. Well, maybe he'd crossed the line a time or two, but he'd honestly tried to do the right thing. He'd practically turned himself inside out trying not to fall in love, and he still didn't know how it was all going to work out, but it was time to act. This could turn out to be the greatest disaster of his life, but he was through pretending he didn't at least want to *try* for a life with that woman.

"Might as well start right now," he said, sliding past his sister and out into the aisle. He covered the distance across to Simone's section and up to where she was preparing to leave with Rina and the aunties in long, space-eating strides. Shouldering Brooks out of the way, he grabbed Simone's hand, saying, "Come with me."

She looked startled, almost frightened. He nodded to his aunts.

"Give us a minute or two, will you? We'll be right over here."

He led Simone just a few paces away to an empty row of chairs and sat her down next to him, then took her hands in his.

"Pray with me."

"Morgan."

"Here and now. If praying in public is going to condemn us, Simone, then so be it."

She glanced around, but then she bowed her head. He did the same, feeling his hair brush hers. A quiet intimacy enveloped them, shutting out the rest of the space and the milling crowd slowly exiting the building.

"Lord," he said, "Simone and I want to be together. It's complicated, but underneath it all, it's really just this simple. I want her, and she wants me. I don't know how to work it all out, but You do. Won't You do that for us? If it can be within Your will for our lives, we want to spend them together."

"Please," Simone added softly, squeezing his hands, and that one small word warmed Morgan as nothing else could.

"In Jesus's Name, amen," he closed.

Afterward, they both smiled, and he kissed her on the forehead. "There. I feel better."

"Me, too."

"See you Friday in class."

"Yes."

"And Sunday in church."

"Yes."

"And next week."

She chuckled. "Yes. I won't skip again."

"Then it's not as gloomy as all that, is it?" They could still see each other and not date. It wasn't as if they'd actually dated to begin with, unless that one dinner after she'd met with her mother counted, and personally he chalked that up to therapy for both of them.

"No. It's not as gloomy as all that."

He got up and let her out into the aisle. Rina had been watching them carefully, but he didn't mind. Let the whole world watch. He wouldn't deny what he was feeling, what was happening between them. What was the point?

She left with his aunties, Rina and Kent, casting him a shy wave farewell as they went out. He gave her a broad grin in return, Brooks standing at his elbow.

"So what are you going to do?" Brooks asked as they started up the aisle together.

"I'm going to lay my career on the line," Morgan answered bluntly.

"Oh, well, you're about ready to retire anyway, aren't you?" Brooks bantered.

Morgan turned a bland expression on his friend and said, "As soon as we reach the sidewalk, I'm going to punch you."

Brooks slung an arm around his shoulders and laughed.

Provost Haward was a busy man, so it was Monday before Morgan could get an appointment with him. He said nothing to Simone or anyone else about it, save his father and Brooks, but he prayed consistently beforehand, so he felt quite calm when he went into the large, well-appointed office. He expected to walk out with an ultimatum or, possibly, without a job, but he'd determined to cross that bridge when he came to it. There were other colleges where he could teach, perhaps not a Bible college, but an institution of higher learning. The thought roiled Morgan's stomach, but he laid it at God's feet and left it.

When Cordés Haward waved him into a chair and said, "Chatam, what can I do for you?" Morgan didn't beat around the bush.

"Sir, I have a problem with a student, a serious one, and I thought it best that I bring it to you, get it out in the open."

"Who is she this time?"

"Simone Guilland."

Cordés seemed surprised. He obviously knew the name, and well he should, given the unusual arrangements made for her tuition and the way she had entered into the program. "She doesn't seem the type. What's she done?"

"She hasn't done anything." Morgan frowned. Then realization dawned. "Oh, it's not *that* sort of problem. She's not chasing me around campus or anything like that."

"Then what *is* the problem?"

Morgan tugged on his ear and said, "The problem is that I'm in love with her."

That rocked Haward back in his plush leather chair. After a moment, he templed his fingers and asked, in all seriousness, "What do you intend to do about it?"

"I intend to marry her," Morgan stated flatly, leaving no room for doubt.

To his surprise, Haward leaned back in his chair, looked heavenward and said, "Thank You, Lord!"

"Sir?"

Haward rocketed forward, leaning over his huge walnut desk. "Do you know how long I've prayed for this day? Every year I hear it! 'Chatam is the biggest distraction on this campus. Why doesn't he just get married? When is he going to get married?' Every year I tell them, the faculty and the regents and the parents, 'Mind your own business. The man's never given us a scintilla of evidence that he encourages these girls to lose their minds over him.'"

"That's putting it rather strongly," Morgan objected. "Losing their minds?"

"I've had girls in the medical clinic crying because you wouldn't pay them attention!" Haward bawled. "There have been times when I thought that if you walked across this campus wearing your motorcycle gear one more time, I'd have to throw you out of here."

Morgan didn't know what to say to that. Modesty seemed to demand that he say nothing, so he clamped his jaw shut.

Haward waved a hand, decreeing, "So marry the girl, and the sooner the better."

"I couldn't agree more. There's just one tiny problem."

Cordés made a face. "Yes, yes, I see. She's a student. And we have rules for a reason."

"I know that," Morgan said solemnly, "and I have tried to live by them, believe me."

"You haven't been seeing the woman?"

"Well, yes, for one reason or another," Morgan said carefully, "*mostly* having to do with my responsibilities as her faculty adviser. Sort of."

The provost closed his eyes. "Let me rephrase that." He pinned Morgan with a very pointed stare. "You haven't been *dating* the woman, have you?"

"No," Morgan answered, "not as such."

Haward lifted a hand. "I'll take your word for it. As I've said, you've never before shown the slightest disregard for the regulations."

Morgan considered saying more and decided to settle for a simple, "Thank you."

"Now," the provost said, picking up his reading glasses and putting them on, as if they would help him think better, "it seems to me that what we have to do is get your young woman on the faculty."

"We thought of that," Morgan admitted, "but someone else was hired for the only staff opening I could find."

Haward sent him a look over the rims of his glasses that seemed to ask, *Who do you think you're dealing with here?* He cleared his throat, leaned back in his chair and mused, "She's in the social services program, isn't she?"

"Yes. She's doing a mission assignment and internship with my father at the DBC youth and young adult mission."

"Ah. And naturally that threw the two of you together."

Morgan fought against a smile at the provost's attempt to make convenient excuses for him. "Naturally."

"Let me see what I can do. There's some talk about needing a coordinator between the Social Services Department and the community."

Morgan was surprised to hear that. "Oh? Who's

talking about that?" Maybe he could put a word about Simone in the right ear.

Haward smiled. "Me. Or I soon will be."

Grinning, Morgan stood, placed both hands flat on the dean's desk and said, "Cordés, thank you. You've been an answer to prayer today."

"My own!" The man chuckled. "Glad to do it. The policies in place are designed to prevent unscrupulous professors from dallying with impressionable young women, Morgan. You simply do not fit that description." He got up and offered Morgan his hand, joking, "Oh, how the mighty have fallen, though. Eh?"

"Like the temple of the Philistines caving in on Samson's head," Morgan admitted.

"I don't think Samson was this happy about it."

Morgan laughed. "I doubt it. But, um, could we keep this between us for the time being? I haven't exactly popped the question yet. I needed to do this first. And there are some other issues. We could still use some of those prayers, if you have any left over."

Haward nodded, escorting him toward the door. "Sure, sure. Best get her on faculty first. Do things in the proper order. The rest will work out."

They shook hands again, and Morgan went out with a new spring in his step. He was perspiring a little, too, and who could blame him?

Was it possible that Morgan Chatam's bachelor days were about to come to an end?

"Oh, Lord," he prayed, feeling a sudden chill, "I hope I'm not making a mistake."

What if she agreed to marry him and then came to regret it, realizing ten years from now that marrying him had been the real death knell to her hopes of one day having a child? He knew that his father would tell him he was borrowing trouble by thinking like that, but he couldn't help it. No man wanted to disappoint the woman he loved, even if the only way to prevent it was to give her up.

Chapter Fifteen

When Simone opened her student mailbox on Tuesday afternoon to find a letter from the provost's office, her first instinct was to panic. Surely someone had told the provost that she and Morgan were seeing each other, which wasn't, strictly speaking, true. Her second thought was to take all the blame on herself, for Morgan's sake. When she read the letter, however, she laughed for sheer joy.

Would she be interested in assuming a position as liaison between the Social Services Department and the community? If so, the department chair would like to speak to her about her duties, specifically coordinating volunteers and interns for various social service organizations in the area. It was perfect, a godsend. Simone ran straight to Morgan's office with the letter in her hand.

She was met there by a plump, freckle-faced,

forty-something redhead who introduced herself as Professor Chatam's administrative assistant.

"Did you want to see the professor?"

Feeling a little foolish, Simone replied in the affirmative. "If it's not too much trouble."

"He's with a student right now, but he'll be free in a few minutes. Would you like a cup of coffee while you wait?"

Looking around at the curious gazes of everyone else in the surrounding cubicles, she hesitated. "Oh, maybe I should come back or see him in class."

Just then, the door to the only real office opened and Morgan came out, followed by a dark-skinned young man in baggy clothes and big glasses.

"Thank you, Professor Chatam," the younger man said in heavily accented English.

"No problem, Burindi. Let me know if that new tutor doesn't work out for you."

"I will, sir, and God bless you."

Morgan smiled at Simone and said, "He already has, my friend. He already has."

He clapped the young man on the shoulder, sending him off, and waved Simone forward. She couldn't help feeling that he already knew what she'd come to tell him.

Waving the letter in her hand, she asked, "Did you have something to do with this?"

"If that's a job offer," he said, grinning, "I might have had a little something to do with it." Leaning in, he told her softly, "I had a—how shall I put this?—*confessional* conversation with the provost yesterday."

"Morgan!" she gasped unthinkingly, alarmed.

"Not to fear. He was very *pleased* to help."

"That's wonderful."

"It is, indeed."

He placed his hands on her shoulders then and turned her to face the room at large, calling out, "Everyone! Everyone!" All the curious faces that had peeped at her earlier now emerged fully from cubicles around the perimeter of the space. "This is Simone Guilland," Morgan announced. "She's joining the BCBC faculty as a—" he grabbed her hand and quickly skimmed the letter "—community liaison. Simone, this is my absolutely essential assistant, Vicki Marble, adjunct instructor, Deon Welch…" He went on introducing the various teachers and workers in his department, about half a dozen in all. Then he simply said to his department staff, "Well, we're cutting out. If you need me, you know how to reach me."

Ducking into his office, he reemerged with a brown leather bomber jacket, which he folded over one arm. The other he looped about Simone's waist.

"So, want to go out to dinner?"

"Morgan!" she hissed, torn between laughing and throwing an elbow into his ribs. "They're all staring at us."

He bent his head and said right into her ear, "Get

used to it, sweetheart. We are, as of this moment, a very public couple."

She laughed delightedly. All the way across campus.

It was so freeing to be with Morgan without pretense or fear of compromising his position with the college. While he drove to the bistro that was quickly becoming their restaurant, she called the head of the Social Services Department and set up a meeting for the next day.

By the close of business Wednesday, she was officially employed, so when Morgan openly took a seat beside her at prayer meeting that next evening, she linked her arm with his and quietly exulted. Rina had intended to come along again, but halfway down the carriage house stairs, she'd decided that she was just too tired.

"This kid hasn't let me sleep in days," Rina had said, holding her belly with both hands. "I think she's dancing hip-hop in here, and my back is sure feeling it."

"Things will probably calm down soon," Simone had told Rina. "She has to be running out of space."

"I suppose that's true," Rina had said. "I sure am." With that, she'd laboriously turned and headed back up the stairs.

This time when the moderator asked Simone if she had any prayer requests, she mentioned Rina and the baby. Then she said, "And I have a praise. I got a job at BCBC."

Over the many congratulations that came her way, Brooks, who was sitting in front of the aunties, twisted in his seat and waggled his eyebrows meaningfully at Morgan, asking, "Any other good news?"

Morgan draped his arm across the back of Simone's chair and said, "We've been dating all of two days. Give a guy a chance."

Simone bit her lip at the titters, gasps and happy exclamations.

"Okay, but you're not getting any younger, you know," Brooks jabbed playfully. "I'm just saying."

Morgan put his head back and groaned, to general laughter. "Doesn't someone somewhere need a doctor? Anyone? Anywhere?"

Someone did, actually, but they didn't know until nearly an hour later. After the prayer meeting ended, quite a few people stopped to congratulate Simone on her new job and wish her and Morgan well. Several commented how happy they were to see Morgan interested in someone. An older woman named Tansy Burdett asked how Simone and Morgan had met. The question did not seem entirely innocuous.

Simone opened her mouth to admit that they had met at the college, but then she remembered. "We met at Chatam House, actually."

"That's right, we did," Morgan said, "and it so happens that Simone is the sister of my cousin Phillip's wife." Again, it was entirely true.

Simone nodded enthusiastically. The woman thawed considerably.

"Is that so? My own granddaughter is married to one of Morgan's cousins."

"Reeves Leland," Morgan supplied. "You remember, the cousin that Brooks and I share in common."

"Oh," Simone said, "the one whose wife is—"

"Anna Miranda," Morgan said.

Simone wisely swallowed the words *trying to have a baby* and said instead, "Ah."

"Mrs. Burdett is a college regent," Morgan told her with a stiff smile. "As, of course, is my aunt Hypatia."

"Of course," Simone murmured, smiling. She offered a hand to the older woman. "It's a pleasure to meet you."

They escaped several minutes later. Once they were safely alone inside his car, Simone having let the aunties know earlier that she wouldn't be riding back to the house with them, she gave him an apologetic smile.

"Oops. I guess I still have to watch what I say."

"No, it's okay," he told her. "Tansy is a stickler, but we haven't really done anything wrong. Besides, Provost Haward would back me, as would many others, or so I have reason to believe. I just don't see the point in roiling the waters unnecessarily."

"I can't argue with that."

They drove up to Chatam House a few minutes later to find an ambulance there, its lights throwing macabre images against the white brick in the dark night.

"It can't be the aunties," Morgan said. "They're standing on the lawn."

"Chester and Hilda, too," Simone noted.

"And there's Carol," Morgan pointed out, identifying the housemaid, Hilda's sister. That just left...

"Rina!" Simone gasped, jumping out of the car.

She slogged through the thick gravel of the driveway. Morgan caught her easily, taking her arm.

"You don't think he found her, the baby's father?" Simone worried aloud.

"I don't know."

They made it to the ambulance just as the emergency medical technician was about to close the doors. Rina spotted her and held out her hands, crying, "Simone!"

Without even thinking, Simone climbed into the back of the ambulance, asking, "What's wrong? What's happened?"

"Premature labor," the EMT answered. "We'll do our best to stop it."

"Oh, Simone, I'm so sorry," Rina said. "I—I just didn't realize."

"It's not your fault," Simone assured the girl,

smoothing hair out of her eyes. "It's going to be all right."

"Will you stay with me?"

"Of course."

"Tell him I'm sorry."

"Who?"

"Professor."

Simone shot a puzzled, anguished look at Morgan. "I'll follow behind," he said. Then he called out to the girl, "Rina, I'm praying for you. We're all praying for you and the baby."

The girl nodded, swiped at her tears, then grimaced and gritted her teeth. The EMT spoke into the radio clipped to his shoulder, pulled the door closed and waved Simone down onto a narrow padded ledge next to the gurney. The ambulance eased into motion, rocking slightly side to side. Simone began to pray silently, but despite all efforts and all prayers, Rina's baby girl was born prematurely at four-forty Thursday morning. She weighed all of four pounds and three ounces.

"Could have been worse," the pediatrician announced when he came out to the waiting room, explaining that the baby was probably less than two months premature. "She's scrawny, but she seems well developed. All the same, given the lack of prenatal care, we'll want to take every precaution."

They would be transferring her to a neonatal unit in Dallas, but the doctor had no problem with Simone snapping cell phone photos and recording a short video of her in her incubator first.

"You can go on into the nursery," he said. When Morgan hesitated, the doctor nodded at him, too, saying, "Just be quick."

Surprised but pleased, they both donned the necessary garb and went in. She was a spunky little thing, pushing at her pink sock cap with both fists and kicking her tiny feet. Simone wished desperately to hold her, but that was not to be, of course. Morgan seemed to sense the need in her and wrapped his arms around her as the nurse whisked the baby away.

"Simone," he whispered, "I want to give you your every heart's desire, but I'm so very afraid that—"

She stopped him, reaching up to press her fingertips to his lips. "Don't," she said. "Someone recently told me that we have to ask for what we want, and we asked to be together, didn't we?"

"Yes."

"Well, then."

He put his head to hers, and they both closed their eyes. "Lord," Morgan said, "somehow I know You'll make a way for us. I must believe it."

"I must, too," Simone whispered.

They shed the nursery gear and walked arm in arm to Rina's room. She was sitting up in bed, eating pudding and sipping a soft drink.

"Have you seen her?" she asked anxiously, pushing away the bed tray.

Simone nodded. "The doctor says her lungs need some development, and she must put on some weight, but so far as they can tell, she's fine."

"I tried to take care of her," Rina said, hanging her head. "I guess I didn't do a very good job. I hope you're not disappointed in me."

Simone glanced at Morgan. "I'm very proud of you, Rina. You did the best you could under very difficult circumstances. And she's fine. You'll be released from the hospital in a day or so, and I'll take you into Dallas to see her. I'm sure they'll let you hold her. I read somewhere that babies thrive best when they're cuddled."

"Oh, no," Rina said, shaking her head. "I couldn't. Anyway, I've already called my aunt up in Missouri. That lawyer found her for me. She's coming down to get me, and I'm going to stay with her, maybe go to college up in Springfield. She says there's a few Bible colleges up there."

"I'll write you a recommendation, if you like," Morgan offered, and Rina beamed.

"That would be cool. I'll take you up on that."

Simone's heart was breaking to think that Rina would never even hold her child. She knew it was probably for the best, but still…if that had been her own little girl, no power on earth could separate her from that baby. She pulled up the photos on her phone and handed it to Rina, asking, "Don't you even want to see her?"

Rina took the phone and thumbed through the photos. "So tiny," she said in an awed voice. "She's pretty, though, don't you think?"

"She's beautiful," Simone told her. "There's a video."

Rina played the video, smiling. "I told you she was a mover and a shaker."

Simone chuckled. "You did."

Rina watched the short video again and thumbed a tear from her eye before handing the phone back to Simone. "So what are you going to name her?" she asked.

For a moment, Simone did not react. The question made no sense. She thought she'd misheard. Then Morgan said, "What?"

Rina looked from one to the other of them. "I just thought I'd ask. It's okay if you don't want to tell me."

Something started inside of Simone, a glowing, trembling, shattering pinprick of light, a stunning, joyous, unbelievable hope, the tiniest tip of a realization. Morgan put his hands on Simone's shoulders and stepped up very close, his feet bracketing hers, his chest pressed to her back.

"Rina," he said carefully, "why would we be choosing a name for your baby?"

She shifted her gaze back and forth between them. "She's not *my* baby. She's *your* baby."

Simone would have fallen to the floor if Morgan

hadn't wrapped his strong arm around her waist. "Rina!" she gasped. "What are you saying?"

"Didn't that lawyer tell you? I said it straight out from the first. I could look the world over and not find better parents for her than the two of you. He said you might not get married, but I knew you would. You are, aren't you?"

"Yes," both Morgan and Simone said at the same time. They hadn't even spoken of it, but in her heart of hearts, Simone had known they would. Still, she rejoiced to hear Morgan's voice in concert with hers.

"But, Rina," Simone asked, tears streaming down her face, "are you sure you want us to adopt your baby?"

"I never did feel this was my baby," Rina said, "just that I couldn't kill it, that it had a right to live. Then that night I came to you at the mission when you told me about your cancer, I knew this baby was for you. I'd've given her to you even if you and the professor hadn't got together for good."

"You know, Rina," Morgan said carefully, "most adoption agencies would feel that I'm too old to raise an infant."

Rina waved that away. "My dad was fifty when I was born. He's taking care of my mom and my grandma now."

Simone had to smile at Morgan. "May we call age a dead issue, never to be raised again?"

For answer, Morgan bowed his head, pressing

his face into the hollow below Simone's ear. "Sweet Lord," he prayed softly, "forgive me. I never even dreamed—I never even *dared* to dream—that You could bless me so. No wonder it took so long! What a blind, stupid—"

Simone lifted her hand to the back of his neck, interrupting that litany. "You are speaking of the father of my child," she burbled, laughing and weeping all at once, "not to mention the man I love."

"Sweetheart," he said, turning her to face him, "I cannot tell you how much I love you, but I'll try. Every day for the rest of my life, I'll try."

"I will hold you to that, Professor Chatam," Simone exulted, lifting her arms around his neck and hugging him.

"And, Rina," he said to the girl in the bed, "thank you. We'll give our girl the very best possible life."

"I know that," she said. "I know all about you from your cousin, the lawyer, but I saw it all that day at the amusement park. You're just the kind of people I want for her. You're the kind of people I want to be."

"What a lovely thing to say," Simone told her.

"There's just one kind of person to be, though, Rina," Morgan said, "and it starts with a personal relationship with Jesus Christ."

Rina nodded. "That's what the Worths said and that Miss Chatam. They've prayed with me, and I figure I'm on my way."

"I'm so glad," Simone said. "We'll stay in touch, won't we?"

"Sure. I'd like that. Shouldn't you be going, though? Seems to me you've got some things to do. I told the hospital that you were the parents and you and the lawyer would be taking care of everything."

No wonder the pediatrician had reported to them and let them into the nursery so easily!

"I'd better call Asher," Morgan exclaimed.

They hugged Rina and parted with tears and smiles. Simone felt that she was floating through the hospital corridors and out into the parking lot.

"Talk about getting the cart before the horse," Morgan said with a laugh. "It isn't just that we have a baby and we're not yet married!"

Simone stopped in her tracks and covered her lower face with her hands, her eyes wide as the implications sank in. "Oh, this is one family circumstance that's going to take a lot of explaining."

"I think the soonest possible wedding date is the best possible answer, don't you?"

"I do."

"Halfway there," he teased. "Thanksgiving is in a week. Good time for a honeymoon."

"Or to set up a nursery," she countered.

"Speaking of that, you've barely even seen the house. We also need to hire a nanny. I'm sure there must be home studies and things like that, too, even in a private adoption."

"Where to begin?" Simone asked, her mind awhirl.

"How about if we head into Dallas to see our little girl first?" Morgan suggested. "Maybe they'll let us hold her."

Simone threw her arms around him. "Yes, please." He grinned down at her.

"What are we going to name her, anyway?" he asked, turning Simone toward the Beemer in the lot. "My mother's name was Ardis Clara, a bit old-fashioned. My stepmom was Kathryn Ann. I like that, but I suspect my sister will want to use it, although I did beat her to the punch, so to speak." He shook his head. "I still can't believe it. I'm a father, and I'm about to be a husband. Have I told you that I love you?"

Simone laughed. "Yes, but please keep doing so."

"I love you."

"I love you, too," Simone said, coming to a halt in front of the car. "I was thinking of Brigitte. For a name, I mean."

Obviously surprised, he took her face into his hands, his warm brown eyes glowing. "She deserves that, and I would like it very much. So would Brooks, I think."

Simone smiled. "Brigitte it is, then."

He took her into his arms and kissed her, there on the sidewalk in the very early morning on that chilly November day when God answered all their prayers and showed them just how complete and far-reaching His plans for His children could be.

Afterward, as Morgan handed her down into the car, he said, "You know, we might need a minivan."

Simone snorted with laughter. "For one small child?"

"Well, maybe a station wagon," he said, closing the door. Then as he came around to drop down behind the steering wheel, "Or a sport utility vehicle."

"Why not all three?" Simone quipped.

"There you go," Morgan said. "We'll just trade all three existing vehicles."

"And what of the moped?"

"No," he said, starting up the engine. "No moped."

"And the motorcycle?"

He made a face as he backed out of the parking space. "I guess that a husband and a father does have some responsibility when it comes to his personal safety, so…actually, I don't think I need the motorcycle anymore."

"In other words," she teased, "you've finally grown up."

"Maybe not completely," he said, shifting gears and laying down a little rubber, just because he could.

Simone laughed indulgently and said, "There are always roller coasters."

"Sweetheart," he said, "I'm on one, and I don't ever plan to get off. You're all the thrill I need from now on."

Simone closed her eyes. There were thrills and there were thrills. Some lasted only long enough to shock and rattle. Some could be clutched close for bright, heady hours. A few burrowed into the heart and lasted a lifetime. After all her mistakes and misfortunes, God had seen fit to gift her with the latter, and she would never take it for granted, never stop being grateful and never doubt His provision or love.

"I'm a mother," she said dreamily, "and will you look at this, I caught the campus heartthrob!"

Morgan put back his head and laughed with all the joy she felt.

* * * * *

Dear Reader,

Have you ever wanted something desperately and realized that God was not going to give it to you, at least not the way you'd envisioned it?

I certainly have, and I don't mind telling you that it was a crushing disappointment. It was also a lesson in faith, for that something I so desperately wanted that God did not let me have He replaced with something far better than I could have imagined.

That's what I imagined for both Simone and Morgan. Simone wanted to become a mother in the same way that most women do, but God had a plan that was better not just for her but for three other people, as well. Morgan intended to love one woman, who married someone else, but God had a plan that was better not just for him but for *five* other people.

No matter how we imagine them, God's plans are always best!

Arlene James

Questions for Discussion

1. The National Runaway Safeline estimates that on any given night there are approximately 1.3 million homeless youth living unsupervised on the streets of the U.S.A., in abandoned buildings, with friends or with strangers. Does your community attempt to provide shelter for what are often referred to as "unaccompanied" youth?

2. Seventy-five percent of all runaways are female; between 6 and 22 percent of those are or become pregnant while homeless. Can you imagine what it is like to live on the street while pregnant?

3. Seventy-five percent of homeless youth have or will drop out of high school. Can you imagine how difficult it is to attend school while homeless?

4. Teens 12 to 17 become homeless for many reasons. Many run away due to physical, emotional or sexual abuse. Others wind up homeless for economic reasons. Some are aging out of the foster care system. Some are escaping foster care. Homeless shelters often refuse to take them for fear the older residents will prey on them. Do you see solutions to these problems?

5. Great strides have been made in the treatment of cancer, especially endometrial cancers, but many women with advanced cases still find themselves unable to bear children after treatment. How might this impact a newlywed looking forward to starting a family?

6. Lyla Simone obviously suffered from feelings of guilt and low self-esteem. As a result, she assumed that her sister and extended family would be unaccepting of her. Do you understand Simone's feelings? Why or why not? What about the feelings of her sister and family?

7. Does Simone's attraction to an older man make sense in light of her inability to bear children? Why or why not?

8. Morgan had lots of experience deflecting the feelings of young women who wanted to gain his attention. Why was it different with Simone? Did her illness have anything to do with it? Explain.

9. Morgan sincerely tried to obey the letter of the regulations concerning professors and students. The provost was satisfied that he did so. Are you? Why or why not?

10. Many more couples wish to adopt infants in this country than can actually do so. Adoption requirements through normal channels are very stringent, and the process can be very expensive. Private adoptions are handled much more loosely, however. Does this seem right or fair to you?

11. Some believe that biological or natural parents should have no say in who adopts their offspring. They feel that the whole matter should be handled by unemotional third parties. Does this seem right or fair to you?

12. Dr. Brooks Leland married a woman whom he knew to be dying, and he believed that was all part of God's plan for his life. Does that seem possible or reasonable? Why or why not?

LARGER-PRINT BOOKS!

GET 2 FREE
LARGER-PRINT NOVELS
PLUS 2 FREE
MYSTERY GIFTS

Love Inspired®
SUSPENSE
RIVETING INSPIRATIONAL ROMANCE

Larger-print novels are now available...